THE INCREDIBLE ADVENTURES OF TOBY FARRIER

1

The Incredible Adventures of Toby Farrier

Middle-School – Teen Fiction

First published in Australia in 2022 by Probert Consulting

Cataloguing in Publication Data is available from the Australian National Library.

ISBN: (trade paper-back)   978-0-6454178-4-5

ISBN: (E-publishing version) 978-0-6454178-3-8

Website: www.wurugi.blogspot.com.au
Trade enquiries: probertconsulting@bigpond.com

Cover Design: Studio Ink, Bendigo Victoria
        Enquiries: hello@studioink.com.au

Printing: INGRAM

The Incredible Adventures of Toby Farrier

For my grandchildren

Isabella, Annie, Crystal, Millie, Ashton, Henry, Kyamah, Montana and India

You guys rock my world

CHAPTER ONE

Walking through the door to Charlie Ramsay's Sydney Road auction house Toby checked his watch, it was exactly five o'clock. Since moving to the city to live with Pop, he had learnt the importance of being punctual.

'Green skinny leg jeans,' Charlie said as Toby walked in, 'Christmas come early, Tobe?'

'Nope. Mrs Alabaccus wanted me to help her kids with their maths after school. She asked how much, and I said a twenty-dollar gift voucher a week would do it.'

'And the shoes, Nikes, aren't they?'

'Hey, you're pretty switched on for an old bloke, Mr Ramsey,' Toby grinned, yep, the shoes came the same way. Mrs Farah's little girl needs a bit of help with her English, so I coach her with that.'

'It's Charlie, Toby. Jeeze mate, I've told you before just to call me Charlie. It's okay, even in front of your Pop here. I still think of my old dad as Mr Ramsey and it makes me feel old to hear people use it to address me now.'

Toby looked at his grandfather, 'Pop?'

Arthur nodded, 'you know, Charlie was the most fashionable bloke around when we were at school. Always had the latest threads, Omega watch, and ripple sole shoes,' he clapped a hand on Charlie's shoulder. 'Yes, my old mate was one snappy dresser in his day, Tobe.'

Charlie steadied himself against the door and lifted one leg, 'it's still my day, look at the trousers, they came out of an Italian suit,' he waggled his foot. 'The shoes are all leather, and a Pelaco shirt. Mate, I still wear the best.'

'That pullover comes out of another age though,' Arthur laughed, 'but we better not get into who's the best dressed, 'cause it's gunna be Toby anyway.'

'What was it you wanted me for, Pop?'

'Yeah, yeah, I nearly forgot,' Arthur slid off his stool, 'I've done a deal with Charlie to get you a desk. He says you can have a look around, you can have the pick of the place, choose any one you like.'

'Any one? Even the ones in the sheds out the back?'

'Out there too,' Charlie said.

'You sure, Pop? I don't mind working on the kitchen table.'

'I'm sure Tobe, it's time you had a desk anyway. It'll help keep you organised and the house'll be tidier. And when you're famous, you can tell a fawning media, Arthur Farrier gave you your start.'

'Well, if I can have one from any of the sheds, I know exactly the one I want.'

'Do you just? And which one would that be?' Arthur said.

Charlie reached for his keys, 'snib the door Toby, then you can show us,'

Flipping the sign on the door to closed, Toby almost running, led the them to the back warehouse. They squeezed past old tables stacked with chairs and through rows of shelves crammed with items from another era. Some of it was antique and valuable, but to the casual observer most of it was junk. Nearing the back corner Toby pulled back a dust sheet.

'No, sorry not that one,' Charlie shook his head, the loose jowls of his face wobbling, 'sorry Tobe, but I can't let you have it. Better choose something else'

'I don't wish to seem rude, but you did say I could have my pick of the place, and, well I reckon this desk has picked me.'

Placing a hand on his grandson's shoulder, Arthur said, 'don't be ridiculous Son. How could it pick you? And if Charlie says no, then I'm sorry, but it's not for us.'

'If it's not for me, why not? Besides Pop, you did hear Mr Rankin say I could have the pick of the place.' He made quotation marks with his fingers. '*Choose any desk you like*, he said. Well, I like this one.' Pulling a chair out from a table he sat down. 'Charlie, if I can't have it, at least tell me why? Was it your dad's, or something?'

'No, it's nothing like that, more that it's useless.' Charlie ran a hand over the ribs of the roll-top and sighed. 'Been locked from the time it came here. I've never even had a key for it. Look, it'd be better to find something you can use, this thing's just an ornament.'

'Any idea who owned it?' Toby ran a finger around the keyhole. He looked at his grandfather and asked, 'reckon we could open it, Pop?'

'Yeah probably, but cripes boy, you're asking a lot of questions about something you can't have,' Arthur's cheeks were beginning to flush.

Charlie looked through the open door toward the Melbourne skyline and clearing his throat, said. 'We got it from a demo company well over sixty years ago, they were tearing out an old building in the city. Got us to sell off what we could, and dump what was left over. At the end of the auction there was this, a filing cabinet and a chair. And, all matching. The chair's around here somewhere, and the cabinet's in the other room.'

'Sounds good, I'll take them too,' Toby knew he was being rude, but for reasons he couldn't explain, he wanted this desk. Biting his lip he hoped Charlie would forgive him. 'You know, keep the set together.'

Arthur glared at Toby, 'come on Son, don't push your luck, lad.'

Toby's hopes fading, he watched his grandfather turn to face Charlie, open his arms and turn his palms up. They stood facing each other for what seemed like an eternity before Toby heard him say, 'now Charlie, you did say he could choose any desk... So, come on mate, what do you say?'

'I know, I know, and a deal is a deal,' Charlie appeared to be glued to the spot. He opened and closed his mouth as if searching for the right words, 'Toby, I'm a man of my word, but mate, this one's a wreck and there are plenty of better, more modern desks out the front.'

'Yeah, I know that too, but this is the one I want. I reckon it's a lot like I was... you know when I came down to Melbourne and live with you,' Toby said looking at his grandfather. 'I know it's in need of some work, but I reckon you can help me straighten it out. Just like you did with me...'

Hoping his reasons were sound, he asked again, 'now Pop, are you sure we can't, have it?'

Remaining silent, Arthur looked to be deep in thought.

Toby waited, watching Charlie stroking his chin, thinking Charlie had to be reminding himself to shave tomorrow.

'Okay, it's yours,' Charlie broke their silence, 'but getting it out is up to you. Come in after school tomorrow and you better bring a couple of mates who can help with the lifting.' Shaking his head, he turned and started to leave. 'And when you take it home, you'd better use the piano trolley.'

CHAPTER TWO

Grunting and cursing with plans to clean it after dinner, Toby's friends helped move the desk into Charlie's showroom. As they did some Friday nights and because it was Arthur's birthday, Charlie had ordered pizza from the takeaway up the road. Arthur brought a cooler packed with beer for him and Charlie and soft drinks for Toby and his friends. Sophia's mum arrived, surprising Arthur with a cake and candles. Arthur flipped a cloth over an unsold table and Charlie helped him arrange chairs. The old men sitting at either end of the table.

The night reminded Toby of other nights when his friends and their parents would drop in. His grandfather and Charlie had been having their Italiano nights every other Friday ever since Charlie's wife Elsie died and now their little group had grown. There could be up to fifteen people gathered around the old piano. Charlie playing, everyone dancing, and after a couple of beers Arthur would be singing his favourite Elvis, Roy Orbison, or Johnny O'Keefe tunes.

'Hey Mr Farrier,' Sophia said pulling her pouty, help-me-please face, 'how about singing Happy Birthday first and then you can cut your cake.' She started to sway, chanting, 'We want cake, cake, cake. We want cake.' Before long everyone, including Arthur, was joining in.

Charlie pumped out *Happy Birthday* on the piano, and Sydney Road shoppers walking past looked in through the windows with amusement.

With dinner done and the birthday cake consumed and the table cleared, most of the parents started saying their goodbyes and drifted away.

Arthur beamed at Toby. 'Okay fella, let's drag the cover off and show the rest of your friends what you've got.'

Toby revelled in pulling the dust cover off his desk with a flourish. It made him feel like a magician revealing a trick. A solidly locked trick.

Running his fingers down the ribs of the roll top, Ben winked at Jack and said, 'I could play washboard while Mr Ramsay plays the piano.

'Don't be a goose,' Nathan said drooping an arm of his friend's shoulder, 'your timing's worse than mine and everyone knows I'm always late.'

Making faces at his mates Jack sniggered and brushing his hand along the ribs, asked, 'would you want it Soph?'

'Yeah, I reckon I like it and when Toby and Mr Farrier get it all done up, you'll all be envious,' she crossed her arms and pouted at them, 'you'll see.'

'Let's get it open,' said Ben tugging at the handles, 'got a key Tobe'

'Nope.'

'You bought a desk you can't open,' Jack was laughing at his friend, 'only you Tobe, only you.'

'What's that supposed to mean?' Sophia jumped to Toby's defence.

'It's okay Soph, we don't have a key that's all,' he turned to Jack, 'if you think it's about Slasher, you're wrong. He's a turd that's all, nothing more to discuss.'

Taking the top off a beer Charlie said, 'tell you what, if you young fellas can get that open, I'll tell you a yarn about the bloke who's supposed to have owned it.'

'How about telling us while they give it a try?' Arthur said. 'I'm a bit deaf, so you'll have to speak up a bit too.'

'Come on Mr Ramsey,' Jack said, 'we know Toby'll get it open anyway, and besides we all have to head home at nine thirty.'

'Yeah, come on,' said Ben. 'And while we're a listening, we'll be watching old Toby here. He'll be a rubbing and a polishing so much that,' he made a sweeping hand gesture, 'poof, a genie will pop out asking for his three wishes.'

Sophia touched a finger to her cheek. 'And just what sort of wishes would they be, Tobe?' She paused before adding, 'reckon you could give me one of them?'

'S'pose, I only need the one, so you lot can fight over the other two,' Toby winked at her and imagining his friends trying to decide how to divide two wishes four ways, smiled to himself.

'Aha, but you haven't told us what you'd wish for yet,' she pressed him for an answer, 'I think your wish would be to become a writer and probably one as famous as JK Rowling.'

Not wanting to answer her, Toby looked for somewhere to put the dust sheet.

'Here, give me that,' Charlie took it from him, 'I've got some rags and furniture polish around here somewhere.'

Charlie disappeared briefly and returned with an armful of rags and a bucket. In it was a bottle of Brasso, four touch-up pens, and several solvents and polishes.

'I'm going to be keeping an eye on you,' he said passing Toby a cloth, 'so you don't ruin the finish. Now, get started with the damp cloth first.' He flicked a rag over a spot on the top and pointed, 'now it's better you work with the grain and not put too much pressure on it. Gently, gently.' Handing over a bunch of keys, he said. 'There are some more of these hanging above the shelf on the back wall. You might find one that'll do the job among them.'

'Couldn't we just jemmy it open,' Nathan said tossing a can of soft-drink to Ben.

'While you're there, Nath.' Charlie said, 'pass Arthur and me a beer and while I'm wetting me whistle,' his voice changed down an octave or two and he had a spooky quiver to it. 'I'll tell you the story of Private Detective Shamus O'Toole and his desk.'

Dragging a church pew closer, Sophia sat down and sorted keys out in order of size along its base, making it easier for Toby to try them in the lock. She turned to Charlie saying, 'is it creepy? I hope so. ome on tell us your story, Mr Ramsey, and?'

'No, not creepy, more mystery than anything. I came by the desk back in the sixties, a bank had bought a couple of small office blocks. They ripped them down to make way for that monstrosity on the corner of Collins and William Streets. The guy pulling the place down asked me to sell the salvage.'

'You'd better tell them what you mean by *salvage*,' Arthur said.

'We understand salvage, Pop,' Toby said and stood up. 'None of these keys fit. Reckon I'll try that other bunch now.'

'So, we know who owned the desk way back when,' Nathan said, 'but you said something about a mystery.'

'Do you know why it's been kept locked?' Ben was on his back in between the pedestals and looking under the desk shouted.

'I've got no idea why it was locked, but they found it bricked up behind a false wall in the basement. O'Toole died somewhere around nineteen thirty-eight, and as a result, his work died with him. It's my guess that he's the one who locked it. He had no heirs, so I guess the company he rented the rooms from, packed his stuff up and put it into storage.' Charlie looked up at the ceiling and sighed.

Toby was sure there was something else going on in Charlie's mind.

Charlie looked back at them. 'I've always thought that one day I'd get a locksmith in, but never got around to it. Roll-tops were out of style back then and it didn't sell. It's been out there until now.'

Arthur pointed to a blemish Sophia had missed. 'I remember the old man talking about O'Toole when I was a kid. Apparently, he was a pain in the backside for both bent coppers and white-collar crooks.'

'Really?' Toby said, 'I'll Google him when I get home.'

Sophia tapped the lid of the desk, 'I'll race you Toby-boy, and I'll bet you, I can find out what O'Toole was doing before you get this open.'

'You're on,' Toby said, tryinh another key.

'It's getting late, Tobe,' Nathan said. 'Are you gunna keep trying to unlock it here, or take it home?'

Toby looked at his watch, 'I reckon if we use the piano trolley, we can walk it up the street tomorrow. That okay with you Charlie?'

Ben straightened and stretched his arms to get the stiffness out. 'If you want, I can come over after nine, we could do it then. Are you coming too, Nath?'

'Can't tomorrow, Dad's organised a trip to the Aviation Museum. Says we don't do enough as a family, I don't know why though, because if the cricket was on, he'd be down at the MCG,' he shrugged, 'probably 'cause it's free to get in.'

'Getting back to O'Toole, Pop? Why was he such a pain to the cops?' Toby asked, 'was he crooked?'

'Crooked? No way,' Charlie said. 'But he was something of a playboy detective. Not a copper, an investigator. Think, Miss Phryne Fisher from TV. People would engage him to find fraudsters, you know, someone who may have deceived a relative into changing a will. That kinda thing. He must have done alright though. Raced cars, played polo, and I think he even kept a biplane out at Essendon.'

'It would take a shed load of cash to do that today,' said Arthur. 'I can't think of anyone who'd afford it.'

'So, they just left this?' Ben said. 'no one cared?'

'No one to care, I suppose,' Arthur said. He put his hand on Charlie's shoulder, 'but that doesn't tell us why you didn't want to let the desk go, mate?'

'Sentiment, I guess. It's been here over half a century, and I suppose every time I saw it, I thought of Shamus. I liked to think that me giving him a thought now and then, meant he wasn't forgotten. You see, I haven't got anyone either; so, we're kindred spirits from different times, I reckon. Call me crazy, but it's who I am.'

Sophia put her arms around his neck and kissed his cheek. 'I won't forget you, Mr Ramsay, and neither will Jack, Nathan or Ben. Toby'll write about our Friday night pizza parties. And when I have kids, I'll call one of them Charlie, after you.'

Nathan laughed saying, 'I've heard you tell that to other people too, Soph. If you have a kid for every name you've promised, there'll be hundreds of little Nguyens running around.' He crawled around the floor making baby noises.

Ben joined him, crawling in circles at her feet. 'I can see Toby as the babies' dad?' he said.

Arthur stood. 'Okay you lot don't need to worry about any of that rubbish for now. It's a lovely thought though, Sophia, and I'm sure you'd be chuffed, eh Charlie?'

'I dunno? If she does, I s'pose I could leave all of this to her.' Charlie laughed and waved his arm around. 'She can have all the rats and spiders that come with the place too.'

CHAPTER THREE

Jack, Ben, Toby and his desk, rounded the corner to find the Slater Street Gang blocking the footpath. Slasher, in front of them, legs apart, arms crossed. Toby allowed the trolley he'd been pushing to roll until the desk touched the belt buckle of his nemesis.

'Where do you twerps think you're goin'?' Slasher said.

Freckles, number two in the gang, pointed at the large covered object on the trolley. 'What've we got here then? Some kind of piano?' His sneer through chipped and yellow teeth usually worked, but not today.

Slasher glared at Toby and lifted a corner of the dust cover. 'Looks like our bookworm's got himself some kind of old fashioned desk.' He shoved it, but Toby kept his grip on it. The desk rattled but did not move. Slasher gave it anther rattle and stepped back. 'It's so bloody ancient, who'd want it anyway?'

Slasher shadow boxed in circles around Toby and his mates. They ducked and weaved as he taunted, jabbing at them with an open hand. Toby held his ground.

Slasher flicked Ben's ear.

'Rack off.' Ben said rubbing it.

'Wouldn't you reckon Farrier's mum and dad would get him a new one?'

Jack ducked his head as Slasher circled, grinned and circled again. The gang stayed quiet. When Slasher passed Toby, he spun back, grabbed Toby by his shirt and pulled until their noses touched. Toby held the stare.

Slasher pushed, and Toby crashed back into the desk. Again, something rattled inside, only louder this time.

'Let's see what's in it.' Freckles grabbed the cover and threw it aside.

'Back off.' With all his weight behind his shoulder Toby shoved Freckles off balance, smiling when he crashed onto his backside.

Slasher pushed Toby away and extended his hand to Freckles saying, 'It's not worth it, Freck,' and helping his friend to his feet addressed the gang. 'Like I said, Farrier's Old's don't care about him.' Freckles rushed forward and with both hands shoved Toby's chest. Toby fell back onto the desk again, a different rattle this time.

Slasher pushed Toby aside and pulled at the handles of the roll-top, nothing moved. 'Got the key, Farrier?' he said holding out his hand.

'Like that'll happen.' Toby pulled him away.

Slasher pulled his hand back and aimed to punch the lock.

Toby stepped between him and the desk. 'Leave it.' He glared at Slasher

Slasher stepped back, and laughed. 'The bloody thing's locked, not only is it old, it's old and useless. I dunno who thought you had a few brains Farrier, but I reckon they were very much mistaken.' He looked to his gang for the laugh. 'Who owned it... Adam?'

'P. I...' Ben saw Toby's glare and stopped.

'Pi what? Slasher said. 'Pie maker of Melbourne or something?'

Ben went to open his mouth again, but Jack's elbow struck his ribs and he closed it.

'Just piss off, Slash,' Toby said. 'We're not looking for trouble.'

'Found it though didn't ya.' Freckles obviously wanted to flex his authority in front of the younger gang members.

Toby picked up the cover, shook it and threw it back over his desk. 'We'll see you later, Slash.'

Slasher stepped in front of him again. 'Parents chucked you out years ago, didn't they Farrier?' He faded a punch, but Toby swung his head out of the way. The gang laughed. 'Woke up to the fact that you're nothing but a useless piece of crap, isn't that right Farrier?'

Toby feeling his face grow red resisted his urge to fight. He looked around. The odds weren't great, but if Slash wanted to have a go, he could match him. 'you're telling the story piss-ant. So, I guess you'd know.'

Slasher swung another punch, Toby ducked and crashed into the desk almost knocking it off the trolley.

Freckles and the gang started crowding and shoving Toby's mates. This time Toby grabbed Slasher's shirt and pulled until their noses touched again. 'Think you're oh-so-tough when there's a gang behind you eh, Slash? But you know...' He pressed close to Slasher's ear. His voice sung in a snakelike whisper. 'I wonder...you know, if it was just you and me, just how tough would little Danny Sabo be?' Toby shoved him away.

Slasher's feet pedalled as he tried to catch his balance. He tripped falling back into the arms of the gang.

The gang helped him up. He smoothed his clothes and shouted. 'Any time you want to try me, creep...anytime.' He danced around, shadow boxing again, making noises like a prize fighter. 'You just let me know, Farrier, just let me know.'

'Anyone with half a brain knows that when the odds are even, blokes like you don't have a prayer,' Toby said. He put his hand on Slasher's chest and pushed past. He nodded toward his grandfather at the far end of the street and smiled. 'Got to go boys.'

Freckles stepped away. 'Piss off back to grandpa, freak.'

Grinning, Toby touched Freckles' nose. 'Better put a hat on, fella. I'd hate to see you get burnt, Freck.'

Freckles slapped Toby's hand away and said, 'rack off, Farrier.'

Slasher looked up the street to where Toby had nodded. Arthur Farrier was at his front gate watching them. Slasher glared at Toby, then looked at his mates. 'Let 'em pass, fellas.' He made a sweeping bow with his hand. 'We'll do 'em later.'

The gang parted and Toby pushed the trolley toward home.

CHAPTER FOUR

When they reached Pop, he pointed down the street and said, 'I saw Slasher and his mates giving you a bit of trouble,'

'Nah, Toby had it all under control.' Ben shook Arthur's hand. 'Slash pretends he's a street tough when he's got the gang to perform for, but on his own, he's weak as water.'

'I know how to handle myself,' Toby said.

'Before you take that inside, we ought to try and get it open. I'll back the Magna out, and you can take it up the driveway and try some old keys I found,' Arthur said.

They watched him park the car on the street.

'We could probably force it,' Ben said.

'Yeah, but it's old and we don't want to damage it,' Toby said, 'maybe prise the back off and get into it like that, but only if we need to.'

Arthur walked in from the street, 'okay, push it into the sunlight, and let me have a look at it. Some of these things had secret panels or compartments, I'm surprised Charlie hadn't looked.' He ran his hand over the sides. 'I reckon we can open it,' he said and winked at Nathan. Taking a torch out of his pocket the old man studied its front and sides. 'Give it a shake, Nath.'

Nathan did as he was told and different parts of the desk gave their own little rattles.

'Treasure,' Ben said spreading his arms out, his face all eyes.

'Come on, get it off the trolley so it's safe,' Arthur said, and passed him the torch. 'Toby, you slide in and look up behind the front edges, check if you can see anything, you know, hinges, gaps, or slides.'

Toby dropped onto his back, slid in under the desk and was peering up through a veil of dust. Dead spiders hung from age-old webs. He reached up and plucked at the plywood backing. 'There's a piece of paper hanging through this crack, but it's caught on the nails and won't come out.'

'The trip home probably moved it; we'll get it out later.' Arthur said and reaching over, pointed to the back. 'Ben, how hard would it be to prise this off?'

'It's in behind an edge, how do they call it?'

'Rebated?'

'Yeah rebated, but if we use a screwdriver or something and lever it in around the edges, it'll come off.'

'Reckon it's best to leave it for now,' Arthur said and asked, 'what about you Tobe, found anything?'

Toby grunted, 'Got it.'

Ben with more than a hint of excitement in his voice asked. 'What have you got there, Toby-boy?'

Toby twisted a brass lock hidden behind the plinth. It was ornate and shaped like a butterfly. As he turned it, two distinct clicks came from each side of the desk, He was sure it signalled the release of a catch. He slid out and tried to pull the panel toward him. It didn't budge. Toby shook and pushed it in, he tried every way, but the panel stuck fast. 'And I thought I had it too,' he said slumping down onto the veranda step and putting his head in his hands.

'You want me to try?' Arthur said.

'I still reckon we ought to break the lock.' Ben said.

'Not so fast fellas,' Arthur said. 'Toby, get in there and twist that brass butterfly again, and Ben, you listen to the front panel, see if you can hear where the noise is coming from.'

They all listened for the clicks.

'Okay, Toby again,' Ben said, 'and again,' he was grinning so much he looked like a carnival clown. 'Yep, one click at the top on the right, and another one at the bottom, on the left.'

'What do you reckon Pop?'

'We're getting there,' Arthur said. 'Now Ben, if you push in at the top and pull out the bottom, kind of twist it. But be careful not to strain it too much.'

An audible click, and they saw the roll top quiver; it cracked open about a millimetre. Toby had his hands on the handles in a flash. He tried to lift the beaded top back. It didn't move. He felt his frustration build, and fighting to keep his anger under control, had to walk away.

Arthur called after him. 'Shamus wasn't going to give his secrets up easy son. So, there must be something in here, something important enough for him to hide. Whatever it is, it's been there for over seventy years, and you are closer now than anyone else has been in that time. Twist the butterfly again and see what happens.'

'We might lock it again.' Toby walked back to his desk.

'Or we might not,' Arthur said. 'Come on lad, try it again.'

Toby twisted it back to the vertical, this time they heard more clicks. He pushed it back the other way, and from the right side of the desk, a drawer popped open. Twisting it to the horizontal and this time a drawer on the left, opened.

'I told you we had treasure,' screamed Ben, sliding the right hand drawer open and claiming a roll of notes. His face dropped, 'damn, it's only Monopoly money, not much to show for all your trouble Tobe.' He passed the roll to Arthur.

'It's not play money Ben. They're the notes Shamus would have used, and these are the big ones, ten pound notes equal to twenty dollars today. You see, we didn't get decimal currency until nineteen sixty-six. This is a pretty big wad, better count it and see how much is there?' Arthur passed it back.

'You want to count it, Tobe? Ben said.

'No thanks mate, can you and Nathan do it? I reckon we should give it back to Charlie anyway.'

'Count it first and then I'll call him,' Arthur said and turning back to Toby asked, 'now what have you got there?'

'An old book.' He held up a worn volume in one hand and in the other he held a key. 'And I think this must be the key for the top.' He rummaged through the assortment of odds and ends.

Arthur wriggled the key into the front of the panel, but it twisted easily without turning a mechanism. He closed the lid of his toolbox and sat on it. 'Maybe it's a key for something else. Try twisting the wooden handles on the roll top plate.' Arthur could feel his own interest building. 'I'll go and phone Charlie. I reckon he'll want to see this.'

Toby was kneeling, his head between the desk's pedestals and without looking at his grandfather, asked, 'you want me to wait until he gets here?'

'Until who gets here?' Charlie tapped Toby's foot with his.

Toby jumped, banging his head. Arthur, Nathan and Ben burst out laughing.

'I was sitting in the window and thinking about how you blokes got the better of me,' Charlie said rubbing his hands together, 'and knowing you'd be getting into old Shamus's treasure trove, I was so curious that I decided to shut the shop early. Besides I reckoned Artie might have a beer on offer. Thought we could sit back and watch you young blokes tear your hair out trying to open it.' He wiped the back of his hand over his mouth. 'Phew, a bloke could die of thirst in this sun,' he rubbed the sweat from the back of each hand with a tissue he took from his pocket. 'About twenty years ago, I tried to open it, wasted nearly a day on it and still didn't do any good.'

'Here you go mate.' Arthur passed him a beer. 'Soft drink in the fridge when you want it boys.'

'Thanks Mr Farrier,' Nathan said, 'but I reckon Toby's nearly got it, so we can wait.'

Toby put both hands on the handles and tried twisting one at a time, first clockwise, then the opposite direction. Nothing.

Charlie said. 'Try them both, but in opposite directions at the same time,' he took a long swig on his beer, 'I remember an old French dresser we sold once, had worked that way.'

Toby tried, but nothing happened. He felt his frustration build and thumped the right handle with his hand. As he did, the left handle spun and exposed a key hole. Toby tried the key, and as it turned, the clicking of tumblers signalled the mechanism unlocking. He lifted, but the top stayed fast.

'Do the same thing again,' Arthur said, 'but on the other side.'

Toby twisted the left handle back and pressed it in. The right handle turned and exposed another keyhole.

'Gotcha,' Toby whispered inserting the key and turning it. Another series of clicks and the top was free.

Nathan pulled three cans from the fridge and passed them to his mates.

'Toby said I should give you these, Mr Ramsey.' Ben handed over the wad of notes.

'How much is there?' Charlie asked.

'I counted one hundred ten pound notes, and Nath said there's a hundred of the five pound ones too.'

'Fifteen hundred pounds, well I guess they're Toby's,' Charlie said. 'It's his desk, and I reckon we should try Saul down in Elizabeth Street, he trades in old notes. He'll give you a valuation, or he might even offer you a price for them, Tobe.'

'You don't want them?' Toby said.

'Nope, they're yours mate. Be a bit of a help to get your career started.'

'What, why don't I just bank it?' Toby wondered why Charlie would want to ask Saul.

'Hell no…' Charlie waved his hands as if he were damping out a fire. 'I'll talk to Saul on Monday. I'm sure old notes like these are worth more than their face value, and he'll know.' He tossed the wad up and down a few times, catching it as he would a tennis ball, 'I'll see if he'll catch the tram out. If not, come in after school Monday and we'll go to see him. That's if Artie can mind the shop.'

Arthur, put his can to his lips and gave a thumbs-up.

Charlie made a signal to gather everyone in and said, 'it's not as safe around here as it once was, so it'll pay to keep this quiet, at least until you know what they're worth.'

CHAPTER FIVE

Toby imagined the way his desk would look when the room was finally as he wanted it. On Arthur's advice, he decided to get the filing cabinet and chair sometime next week. He put some of his treasures on the sideboard, three broken pocket watches, a pair of cufflinks and a few old photos. Other odds and ends one would expect to find in an old desk, he dropped into a shoe box. He sat at the desk and opened a spectacle case. It contained a pair of wire framed, circular lensed glasses. They were the spring type without arms, he had seen similar worn by John Flynn on a twenty-dollar note. Shaking the case to get rid of fluff that gathered in the corners, the lining opened and a small key dropped out. It made a ringing sound as it bounced onto the floor. Toby studied it for a while, his desk was continuing to give up even more of its secrets?

He went into the laundry and dragged out the machine he knew well: the vacuum cleaner. It wasn't that he liked cleaning, but it was part of his deal with his grandfather. With that and a few other chores, Toby picked up a bit of pocket money every week.

'Hey, be careful with that,' Arthur said as Toby passed the lounge doorway. 'You don't want to suck the pile off the baize, you'd do better using a soft paint brush.' Arthur tailed him into the study. 'You know, I've been thinking, and reckon we should prise the back off. Let's tighten it up, and give it a proper clean before we put it back together.'

'Yeah, Toby said 'might help it to make another hundred years too.'

Arthur disappeared. A few minutes later, he returned from the shed with a chisel, some other tools and a tube of glue. 'This should do the job.' He passed Toby the tool. 'Slide this in where it's loose and work toward the corner. Take your time, use gentle movements.'

Within minutes the back was off. They picked out some old receipts and a few coins. Taped under a shelf of the right pedestal they found an envelope. Scrawled in red pencil across the front was, *Eagle's Talon*, and on the flap the author had initialled, *SBOT*, in several spots.

Toby pointed to the marks. 'Why would he do that?'

'It was a way of telling if the envelope had been opened. If they didn't line up, you'd know if someone had tampered with it. We can look at it later. Here, help me to brush these webs out and we'll glue the back in.'

Arthur shook an internal bracing strut, and the outside panel of the right pedestal fell off. He picked it up, looked at it and said. 'Toby, it's falling apart while we're watching it. I reckon you should swap this over for something more serviceable. I'm sure Charlie wouldn't mind.'

'Nope, this is the one.' Toby held his hands up and wiggled his fingers. 'Think about all the stories trapped within its layers. We have a typewriter, pens, old papers, a mysterious envelope and now another old book.'

'Old book?'

'Yeah.' He held up the book he'd found earlier. 'When the side fell away, a bible and this book dropped out, and it looks like it's, I dunno, big and old.'

'Here, let me see that.' Arthur opened it up and turned some pages. 'It's a diary; the name in the front says it's O'Toole's, probably his journal. See, lots of notes, times, places and people's names. He kept tab of everything.'

Toby felt his excitement build. 'Come on Pop, let's see if we can shake anything else out of the old box?' He wanted to find everything and discover its history. The desk captured him, and he felt his imagination run wild.

'What did you do to open the side panel?' Arthur said

'I didn't, it just fell apart when you shook it.'

Arthur bent down; his fingers spiderlike as they searched the pedestal's rebate. 'No,' he said and pointed, 'it's meant to come away, see these brass pins in the bottom, there must be a trigger, or a latch somewhere. Something we touched made this side come off, and it makes me wonder if the other side does the same?' Arthur checked the back again and continued, 'Here, let's roll it onto its face. The damn thing has me intrigued too. Now Shamus old mate, just what are you hiding in here?'

Toby put a blanket on the floor, and together they rolled the desk forward, several drawers slid off their rails.

'Whoa, stand her up again Tobe, we'd better take the drawers out and lay them on the floor. Keep 'em in order though, otherwise they'll take you all day to sort out.' Arthur sat on the spare chair and watched as Toby put each drawer along the wall. 'A polish, some soap on the runners, and they'll slide like new.'

With the desk tipped onto its front they checked its construction. The timbers were solid and the left pedestal showed the same brass pins as on the right.

'Built by Colonial Furniture and Fine Woodcarvers, of Elizabeth Street, Melbourne, in Eighteen Sixty-Four...' Toby was smiling at this find. 'The manufacturer's mark says a Major Jeffrey Symes commissioned it. See, glued inside the pedestal is a delivery note and the invoice, there's also an order number and delivery address.'

'Shamus must have got it second hand.'

'And look at this Pop,' Toby's finger was on the note, 'twenty-five pounds, twelve shillings and nine pence. How much is that in today's money?'

'Fifty-one dollars and twenty-eight cents. A lot of money for those days considering a working man would be paid little more than two dollars a week.'

'Would it be an antique?'

'It's over a hundred years old so yeah, it's an antique all right. What has me beat though, is how someone hadn't got it away from Charlie years ago,' Arthur stood up and stretched. 'Anyway, it's yours now. C'mon, let's see if we can get the other panel off, and once we've worked that out, we can put it back together.'

Arthur ran his fingers up and under every ledge, until he found a couple of rods that connected to a trigger below the centre drawer. 'There you go Tobe, when you take the centre drawer out, you can slide this lever and the side panels lift off. By the looks of it, that inlay lifts out too. See how it's sticking up on one corner?

'Yeah,' Toby tried to get a finger nail under it.

'Don't bother now, we can try to do it once we stand the old girl up.'

Some glue, a few tacks and the back was in place. Arthur and Toby rolled the desk onto its feet and moved it against the wall. Toby's interest itched and he needed to scratch it. He wanted to look through what they had found. However, as Arthur left the room, he insisted Toby finish one job at a time.

Toby put the drawers back in the order they came out. The two on the outside had false floors and the centre three had deeper faceplates. The extra depth on each concealed a drawer suitable for small items, like paper clips, coins or valuables.

With every nook and cranny clean, Toby knew his desk looked better than it had for over eighty years or more. He could hear Arthur coming and cleared a path into the room.

Arthur passed Toby a soft drink and said. 'Might be time to give it a break.'

Toby took the drink, watching it fizz as he pulled the ring. 'Isn't she a beauty though? Not many kids my age would have something like this.'

'Nor as expensive,' Arthur ran his hand along the facing. 'Charlie phoned, said he's asked around the antique dealers. They all reckon you have something special and worth a pretty penny too. In the thousands, he says.'

Toby felt his spirits drop. 'What, he wants it back?'

'No, it's yours mate. Told me he thought you might like to know, that's all, and he suggested I increase our insurance. Charlie has a soft spot for you and your friends. Says he hasn't felt this much alive since Elsie died.'

'Yeah?'

'You did that for him, Toby. You and Ben, Sophia, Jack and Nathan. When you kids go around to his place and he cranks up that old piano, he feels young again. He just loves it.'

'We have a good time too, Pop.'

'Yeah, and me too.' He pointed at trinkets from the desk that littered every surface of the room. 'Now what are you going to do with all the stuff?'

'I'll chuck out all the old pencils and junk, but Shamus's typewriter, I thought I could write a story on it one day. You know, old school style. I might even use that paper we found in the drawer, and make copies with carbon paper. Maybe I can write something to shock old Willie a bit.'

'Yes, but first you'd better put what you don't want in the bin, box up all the other stuff and put it in the shed. Charlie said he's bringing some steaks for a barbeque at six. So, do you want to ask the others around?'

'I thought about going into the city with them tomorrow, so I'm fine if it's just the three of us tonight, if that's okay with you.'

'Sure, now get that stuff stowed, jump through the shower, and toss up a salad, eh.'

Toby figured as soon as the old blokes were telling their stories, he would be free to slip back to his study and delve deeper into the mystery that was, Shamus O'Toole.

CHAPTER SIX

His study was now the sanctuary that Toby had planned. Smiling to himself he stared, lost in the ribs of the roll-top. Chuffed, was what Ben would say and that was exactly how he felt. The typewriter intrigued him. What was its significance and the AIF markings? Did Shamus buy it as war surplus, or had someone left it with him? Toby took the cover off and felt for the keys. They worked, he touched the ribbon, but it was too dry to mark the paper, and he wondered if you could still buy them. With no time to worry about that, he looked at the writing under the lid. Someone had printed Lt. Paul Spengler by hand, the ink was faded, but Toby felt its pull, challenging him to learn more about Spengler too.

He lifted out the centre insert. Its edges were worn and only a few traces of gold embossing remained. He put it to one side and discovered another bible, this one tied together with a violet ribbon. Something inside it rattled. O'Toole's desk kept adding intrigue. When he pushed the ribbon away and opened it, Toby found a hollow carved close to the spine. It concealed a pen, not a ball point like he used at school, this one had a removable top and a nib. He waited until he heard an advertisement break into the football telecast, and rushed into the lounge room. 'What can you tell me about this?' Toby said and passed the pen to Arthur.

'Haven't seen one of those for a while,' Arthur took it saying, 'Charlie probably still uses one today to write fan letters to Collingwood players.' His elbow bumped his friend's ribs.

'It's a fountain pen. Everyone carried them in the old days. You see Baron Bic hadn't invented the ball point pen yet. Rather than carry around a pot with ink in it and a separate pen, fountain pens were more convenient.' Charlie replied. 'And Artie's right. I still use one for signing letters, etcetera.'

'Here, let's have another Bo-Peep at it.' Arthur said taking the pen back from Charlie. 'It's a bit flash, and heavy too. Do you reckon it's gold plated or brass?'

'Has to be plated, the colour is too good.' Charlie said. 'Brass would be a bit green, even in a dry place. Where'd you find it Tobe?'

'In a bible under the inlay. And why would anyone hide a pen in a bible? This Shamus bloke must have been one secretive dude.'

'There was stuff my parents talked about and sometimes his name would come up. I really can't remember much about it, but something happened. It was around the time of Squizzy Taylor and his like, but O'Toole was on the square. You could always look him up in the library or even try the wed,' Arthur said.

'It's the web, Pop. The internet is called the web, as in spider's web.'

'Yeah?' Arthur started to laugh, 'you could do that then.'

'Artie told me about the typewriter, Tobe.' Charlie said. 'I've got some ribbons at the shop. When you come in Monday, remind me to grab them for you.'

'Ta, I'm going to ask Lord Google about him again, see if I can find out any more.' Toby stopped at the door and turned back. 'Let me know when you are ready to head home, and I'll walk you.'

Arthur put the pen on the coffee table and reached for the TV remote. He clapped a hand on Charlie's knee.

'Thanks for the desk mate, he's going to get a lot of use out of it, aren't you Tobe?'

Toby nodded. 'Did you have any idea about all those hidden panels and things?'

Charlie picked up the pen and studied it. 'I knew the piece was special,' he said, 'but I had no idea about its contents. I wasn't even sure who used it, but knowing O'Toole had owned it at one time, well that made it interesting for me.'

Toby left them and pulled out his laptop. He clicked the search engine icon and typed, *Shamus O'Toole*. Several sites displayed a number of Irish pubs using the title. Facebook held well over a hundred contacts for people with the same name. He dragged out a small notebook and headed a page, *Research – O'Toole*. In the margin, he made notes of things to check out. After an hour of surfing websites, he closed down, grabbed O'Toole's journal and lay on the floor to read it, marking pages with tissues whenever he found something interesting.

He felt a hand shake him.

'Come on Toby, it's nearly midnight,' Arthur said. 'Charlie took a taxi home. You'd better get some shut eye. I'll see you in the morning.'

That night Toby's dreams, confused and wandering, played black and white images in his head.

CHAPTER SEVEN

After a Sunday of chasing O'Toole's history and before recess, an English lesson was the last thing Toby wanted. He was keen to tell his friends about the treasures his desk gave up. In the middle of old Willy's dissertation on dangling modifiers, he leaned over and showed Sophia the fountain pen. She took it and pulled a face at him.

'Feel like sharing with the rest of the class, Mister Farrier... Or do you think you can explain sentence construction to our little gathering better than I can?'

'No sir, sorry.'

'Not good enough Farrier and a glib *sorry* won't cut it. What was so important that you should disrupt the class? I think it only fair that you share with everyone in the room.'

'I was showing Sophia an old pen I found yesterday, I haven't seen anything like it before. Mr Ramsey says he still uses one.'

She handed the item of interest over to the teacher who was standing over her, his hand open.

'Come and see me at the end of lesson, Toby. I'll give it back to you then.' He turned on his heel and walked to the front of the room. 'Right class, because we have had time to think about what has just happened here. I want you to give me no less than one hundred words of free writing, and your story must include the words *fountain, pen and gold*. You have less than fifteen minutes.' The pen shone gold as Willy held it up to the light.

Toby knew the others would be miffed, but he revelled in writing and within minutes he had over two and a half pages of text. Satisfied by the way he structured his story around the three words and that they had at least three paragraphs between each of them. Folding his hands behind his head, he leant back in his chair and waited for Mr Wyatt to collect the papers.

Recess sounded and Slasher flicked Toby's ear as he walked past. 'You're a tool Farrier, and if you ever try a stupid move like that again, I'll fix you for good.'

'Anytime thug.' Toby said without looking at him.

'Toby?' Mr Wyatt was holding the pen toward him. 'This is a lovely early twentieth century writing tool, where did you get it?'

'Pop bought a desk from Mr Rankin, and this was in it.'

'A desk? So, you've taken my advice and created a space to write, that's great. I'll be expecting to see some top work coming from you now.'

Toby wanted to race to the schoolyard, but it could wait a minute. He liked how Mr Wyatt had encouraged him ever since the first day of term. 'Sir, how would I find information about a private detective from the twenties?'

'From the twenties, I suppose you could go to the library and search court reports, newspapers etc. Then cemetery records, they might help. Why, who is it you're trying to find?'

'The bloke who owned the desk was a detective called Shamus O'Toole. I Googled him and found nothing. I just wondered what he looked like, that's all.'

'Good luck,' he pointed to the door, 'your friends are waiting.'

Ben and Sophia stood near the benches waiting for Toby. Nathan came from the area of the drinking fountain wiping his mouth, Jack trailed him.

'Thanks for that.' Nathan shot a killer look at Sophia. 'If you hadn't pulled a face, old Willy wouldn't have seen Toby's pen, and we wouldn't have had to rush out a hundred words in fifteen minutes.'

'What did he go on about when we left the room, have you got detention?' Sophia asked.

'Nah, everything's cool Soph. He just asked about the pen and where I got it. I told him I found it in the desk and asked how to go about finding information on O'Toole.'

'God, I thought you were in for one of those one on one lectures of his, or even worse, detention. You know how quick he is to give either of them if we jack up,' Ben said. 'I know you're his pet and all that Tobe, but anyone else and we would be doing detention for the rest of the week.'

Toby just grinned. They passed the pen around, and before he could tell them everything, the buzzer to finish recess roared.

Slasher bumped his shoulder into Toby's back. 'Don't stuff up again Farrier, or I'll rub your face along the footpath, understand'

Slasher was older than Toby but they shared classes. Slasher's performance had kept him back a couple of years during his schooling. It wasn't that he was stupid in an academic sense, however, trouble made him a close companion. Making high grades were of low priority to Slasher Sabo.

Walking away, he said, 'after school, idiot.'

'After school yourself turnip...' Toby yelled at Slasher's back.

At lunch, and between their afternoon classes, Toby told his friends about the things he found in the journal. He was particularly interested in the sealed envelope, as its contents didn't make a lot of sense to him.

Sophia said, 'I could set up a database, you know, try a few different things with times and place names to see if I can find a pattern. Would that help?'

Nathan nodded. 'And if we take a trip to the library, like old Willy suggested, we might find something there too.'

'Charlie has told me I can pick up the chair and filing cabinet this arvo, anyone want to help?'

The friends all agreed to meet at Charlie's no later than four o'clock.

CHAPTER EIGHT

Rounding the corner, Toby and Ben watched their teacher's old Red MG driving away.

'What's old Willy been doing at your place, Tobe?'

'Don't know, I thought everything was okay when we left school. Anyway, if I'm in trouble we'll know soon enough, come on we're nearly there.'

'Yeah, you did say he was okay at recess.'

'He was, wonder what he wanted?' Toby pushed a drawer closed and shook his head trying to rid himself of unfounded guilt.

Until now the trip from Charlie's had been uneventful apart from the bottom falling out of the top drawer of the cabinet. Papers stuck out of the back, but hadn't fallen. The boys expected Slasher and his mob to confront them at some stage, but nothing happened.

Arthur was pleased to see them return. Circling the filing cabinet, he whistled, shook his head, pulled the bottom drawer, raised his eyebrow and said, 'got yourself a doozy here Tobe, if you didn't want it to fall apart on the way home, you should have taken my rubber tyred trolley.' He clapped a hand on Toby's shoulder, 'your English teacher has been here.'

Before Toby could answer Ben offered, 'yeah, we saw him drive off. What did he want?'

'He left you a note. Says he knows someone who might be able to help with the history of your desk. What surprised me was that you kept Shamus' name from him. Why do that?'

'He seemed more than a little interested in the pen, and I wondered why? If Shamus had a reason for keeping his desk locked, then maybe it should stay a secret. At least until we know what's in here,' Toby said, tapping the top of the filing cabinet.

Ben slumped into the chair he'd been pushing. 'What do you reckon Tobe, suit me or not?' He stretched his arms out and put his feet up on the filing cabinet.

'You wish, maybe I'll dedicate a page to your help and the grace with which you gave it in my autobiography, *Friends I met on my way to fame*.' Toby put an arm around his shoulder, squeezed and laughed. 'But it'll be my last, so it's years away yet.

'That'd be right. Publish it when I'm dead.' Ben was laughing. 'Come on let's get it inside.'

'Not so fast. You'd be better to sort it out and fix the bottom of that drawer first. Give it a clean and then take it inside.' Arthur was right, it would be better to repair it in the shed.

The key Toby found in the glasses case fitted the filing cabinet lock. Papers lost for decades had collapsed in their folders and littered the drawers.

'You're getting good at this now,' Ben said, 'you sure you don't want a career as a locksmith?'.

'Writing about breaking and entering would be more fun, don't you think?'

'Not me, I'm not cut out for a life of crime and I'm no good at words. So I reckon I'll get a factory job or something.' Ben posed, giving the impression of sweeping, looking around, and leaning on a broom.

Arthur was laughing at him, 'you could go to acting school,' he said, 'or have a go at stand-up comedy.'

After an hour, Nathan came to check their progress. Arthur was inside making a shepherd's pie for dinner.

Stacks of paper covered the car, the bench and Arthur's wicker chair. The boys had glued and nailed the bottoms into all three drawers. Toby was running a bead of glue around the rebate at the back, when he heard Slasher.

'What have you got there now, bookworm? More junk I s'pose.'

Toby looked up. 'Slash, what the hell are you doing here? If I remember right, Pop told you to rack off last time you turned up uninvited, he told you never to come back again.'

'Yeah, well your old bloke doesn't scare me. You twerps have been whispering and secretive all day. After that writing lurk you pulled today Farrier, I wanted to warn you. Stuff up like that once more, and I'll make sure you'll never do it again, understand?'

'Yeah, so you said at school, but a turnip like you doesn't scare me. In fact, I feel sorry for you Sabo, really sorry. It's a shame someone like you has to hang around with kids you can bully into doing your dirty work. Now get lost before I lose my lolly and see you off.'

Slasher looked back over his shoulder as he left. 'Later Farrier, later.'

'He's a tool,' Nathan said, 'a really mean tool.'

'Not worth thinking about,' Toby said. 'He has it tough though. Think about it, how would you like to be him? Having your dad's drunken and druggo mates all around you. His mum does whatever she has to to bring in enough money for them to survive,'

Nathan huffed and said, 'sucks to be him I guess.'

They watched Slasher strolling out of the gate and heading across the park.

Toby's eyes followed until his adversary was out of sight, 'you know, I don't reckon it'd be that easy being Slasher,'

'You're going soft Farrier,' Ben said, 'the bloke cut you with a broken bottle last year.'

'Yeah and I got in a few good hits too.' Toby felt a smile cross his face. 'He'll never have a straight nose again. Come on, help me shift this into my study and then we can put the files back.'

'My study,' Nathan swirled his hand and bowed. 'Gee that has an air of importance about it. I can see it all now. *Sophia, come into my study, we can discuss the matter there.*'

'Knock it off you two,' Toby said, 'it'll never happen.'

'Do you think Sophia would like to see Toby's study, Nathan?'

'Yes, I do, Ben. I very much think that Sophia would like to see inside Toby's study.'

His friends were having fun at his expense, and although it rankled, Toby was happy to be sharing this with them.

CHAPTER NINE

Toby looked over his pie and played in the gravy with his fork. 'Pop, why would a Uni professor offer to help a kid he doesn't know?' He had read a note that Mr Wyatt had left for him with the details for some professor at Melbourne Uni who wanted to him.

'Not sure mate. What's eating at you?'

'I've got a feeling there's more to Shamus O'Toole than a locked desk. I can't stop wondering what he was working on, or if the professor knows about the money?'

'How could he know about the money, Tobe? And anyway, that wouldn't be much to a professor.'

'Yeah, I know it doesn't make sense, I'll Google him later and then think about it.'

'Better finish your homework first.' Arthur said before asking. 'I saw Slasher outside earlier. What did he want?'

'He's just trying to put the breeze up me and the boys. Without his gang he's pretty harmless.'

'Well if he causes any trouble, you know I'll call the cops.'

'He doesn't bother me, Pop. I can handle him.'

'Just take it easy, that's all. His father's lot have been trouble ever since they moved into Brunswick two generations ago, give 'em a wide berth, that's all. Now you get that homework done and I'll finish up here.'

Toby was sifting papers when Arthur came to the doorway of his study. 'Want a hand with anything, Tobe?'

'Homework's all done. Pop,' Toby asked, 'I don't know where to look first, there's so much stuff here. Where do you reckon I should start?'

'Well I guess you need to work out what it is you want to find,' Arthur said. 'Just love it for what it is. Dump all of these old files in the rubbish and make your own history?'

'I just can't let it go Pop; I feel like there's something in there. Calling out, begging me to set it free and make it right. It's something I can't put my finger on and it won't let me alone. I probably need you and Charlie to help me find out just what it is.'

'Right, first up you need to work out what you've got here. You have holidays starting at the end of the week.' Arthur smoothed a piece of paper and began making a list. He rubbed the pencil behind his ear. 'Yep, I'll see Charlie tomorrow, by then he'll have an answer on your money. We'll look at some of the old newspapers he's been hoarding, see if Shamus was mentioned anywhere.'

'Yeah, I hoped that's what you'd do.'

'What did Google tell you about the professor?'

'Not much, I went through his profiles on social media and he seems straight up.' Toby felt a chill and shivered. 'But I get the feeling there's something weird about him that's all.'

'Okay then, look at things this way. There is an answer to your mystery. Most of the pieces are in there, just like a jigsaw. Even if some of them are missing. Using what we know, we'll be able to see enough of the picture to know what's what.'

'But there's so much stuff.' Toby dropped his head into his hands.

'Well, leave the filing cabinet for now. Go through the diary from the back. Work from the last entry to the first. Sophia said she was going to make up a spreadsheet. We'll try to match any pictures or stories we find about O'Toole' with the dates in his diary. His notes will tell you where and when.'

'Thanks, I can see where you're coming from now. Okay to use the wall as a pin-up board?'

'Only if you promise to patch and paint it when you're finished with all of this.'

'I promise.'

'Okay, but don't spend all night on it, you've got school tomorrow.'

CHAPTER TEN

Toby, tight with nervous energy, strained through maths and science, willing recess to arrive. Last night after talking to Pop he found a few things linked to Shamus. The first item he discovered was a newspaper cutting. Shamus was dressed in a dinner suit, complete with bow tie. He sported a pencil thin moustache and the article said he was attending a gala ball. The beautiful socialite, Miss Zeta Oppenheim was on his arm. Toby crosschecked the date of the ball with the diary notes and concluded work was the reason Shamus attended. He found another diary reference for the same day and a carbon rubbing of a foundation stone or similar. The rubbing was beautiful, an ornate carving of an eagle holding a scroll titled, *ANCIENT ORDER of PENNYWEIGHTS*. Across the top of the rubbing someone had scrawled in red pencil *The Eagle's Talon*. Two days later a further note scrawled into the diary's margin: *find the eagle's talon*. What did it mean?

He passed the photo to Sophia.

'She's pretty, and just look at those jewels, she must be rich.' Sophia stared at the picture.

Slasher loomed from behind. 'Probably fakes.' He held her shoulder and tried to snatch the cutting. Sophia drove her elbow back, its point catching him just above the groin. He doubled over, his body crashing into the spare chairs that surrounded their table.

'You're a bitch Nguyen,' Freckles shouted. 'There was no need for that.'

'For what? Just fell over, didn't you Slash?' Nathan said.

Ben stood guard and Toby extended his hand to help Slasher to his feet.

Freckles puffed his chest out. 'A bit lower, and he'd be trying out for the high parts in the boys' choir.' He sucked in his cheeks and spat. It landed alongside her foot. 'You're a malicious slag, Soph.'

'Oh, and that's not gross...?' Sophia turned to him and said, 'I love you too freak.'

The gang circled them.

Slasher looked and motioned to leave; their English teacher was moving in at a brisk walk, 'You'll keep for later Farrier,' he said turning away.

'You keep saying that. Maybe we should visit you one day.' Toby held his eyes on him, willing him to throw a punch.

'Like I said, your day's coming Farrier. Come on fellas.'

Mr Wyatt stared at the group. 'I saw that, Sophia Nguyen. What would your mother say?'

'She'd probably give me a good talking to, Sir. She'd tell me to be a bit more ladylike, more Vietnamese. And yet on the inside she'd be smiling, knowing that the karate lessons weren't wasted.' Sophia smiled. 'He wanted to take this, and I hadn't finished with it, Sir. Besides it's Toby's.' She pouted her lips and opened her eyes. A couple of eyelid bats and he looked away.

'Butter wouldn't melt in your mouth would it, Soph,' he said. 'Those boys may not walk away so easily next time.'

Toby tried to hide the cutting and other notes from him, but it was too late.

'Did Arthur give you the message I left for you?' the teacher said holding out his hand for Toby to offer up the papers. 'Let's see what you've got there, maybe I can help.

'It's okay sir, I think we've got it covered,' Toby said.

'No trouble, besides I like a bit of a puzzle. Is this the man you're trying to research, O'Toole I think you said? Is that him in the photo? The mysterious owner of your new desk? 'Former owner Sir. I got it from Mr Ramsay who ended up with it years ago, said it was left over from a demolition auction.' Toby felt indignant and not about to share information with outsiders. He liked Willy. The teacher had helped him with his entries for writing competitions, shown him punctuation examples and taught him how to edit properly. In his heart, Toby knew Mr Wyatt was okay and didn't understand why he felt suspicious, but he did.

'Come on, Toby. Give Mr Wyatt a look at what you've got there. You never know, he might be able to tell us something about the bloke,' said Ben.

As his friend was speaking, Toby slid the papers into the manila folder he had brought them to school in.

'Toby, I'm only trying to help, that is why I phoned the professor to make introductions for you. If anyone knows about early Melbourne, it's Phillip Ryan,' the teacher said still reaching for the papers.

Toby's hand held firm. 'But Sir, why would he want to help?'

'You could have a piece of history he's researching, or maybe, it's because he's a teacher too and wants to help. Toby, it's not like you to be so secretive. Why is something so old making you cautious?'

'Sorry Sir, you're right and if I can't trust you, who can I trust?' Toby handed them over.

'Interesting, let me make copies and I'll check it out. Anyway, you need to get on with your work this week and not let thoughts of a treasure hunt distract you, okay?'

'I don't think so, Sir. These are the only copies.'

'Come on Toby, we can go to the staff room now, I'll make spare copies for you and your friends and a set I can use for research. They'll be safe. I promise.'

'Two sets, Sir. One for you, one for me, and only if you promise not to share them.'

'Deal.' Mr Wyatt held his hand out and they sealed it.

Toby's teacher stared at the cutting while the copier whirred into life. 'He's a pretty dapper looking bloke, isn't he? It's a pity the paper didn't have colour in those days, it'd be nice to know if he had red hair.'

'Why would he have red hair?' Toby asked, remembering that at one time his teacher's hair was red too.

'It's just that some of the Irish kids I grew up with had red hair that's all.'

Copying completed, Toby took his copies and the originals and returned to his friends.

CHAPTER ELEVEN

Walking into school with Nathan and Ben next morning, Toby heard his name being called and looked around to see his teacher waving to him. The man looked as if he hadn't slept at all last night.

'Wait here, I'll be right back,' Toby said to his friends. 'Coming Sir.'

Willy wrapped an arm around his shoulder. Toby felt the tremble in his arm.

'Sir?'

'Toby, last night I sent the professor copies of those photos we made.' Willy's voice crackled. 'He says that desk is his property.'

Toby felt anger simmering inside him, a feeling he'd left behind when he came to live with Pop. He started to tremble and tried to choke down his violent behaviour. He remembered how it damaged his family, everyday it haunted him. He took a deep breath and held it.

Glaring at his teacher he said, 'Sir you promised, you said if you made copies, you'd keep them safe and you haven't. Now you're telling me some jumped up bloody professor says the desk is his, and it's all because you showed him photocopies of clippings that I only wanted to share with my friends. Tell him to go to hell, it's mine.'

'Toby...' there was caution in Sophia's tone

He ignored her and attempting to withhold his anger, screwed at the pavement with the ball of his left foot. 'Sir, you couldn't even keep your promise.' Toby's hands were shaking. He wanted to pummel his English teacher, but instead clenching and unclenching his fists, said. 'I trusted you...'

'Toby, you have to understand; I was only trying to help.'

'But it wasn't your place to tell anyone though, was it Sir?' Trying to relieve his tension, Toby kept flexing his fingers.

'I know son, and now the professor wants your desk. Said something about it being of National Interest.' His shaking voice came small and weak. 'However, it could be something more personal than that.'

'No that's just crap, the desk is mine, Pop paid for it fair and square... And if you'd kept your word, Sir, this professor bloke wouldn't even know about it. No, you've dropped us in this mess and now you have to get us out. Tell your suck-hole mate to rack off. Tell him that for me Sir. You tell him that.'

Toby's friends had all taken a couple of steps back.

'Toby, check your language, before I bring you before the headmaster.'

'Sir, we know you won't and we also know who created this mess. Does the professor know who I am, or where we live?' A picture of his grandfather flashed into Toby's mind.

'He only knows you go to this school.'

'Well it won't take him long to find me then, will it?'

'Toby, Phillip is all bluster.'

'Hope your right, Sir. I don't feel good about this. Like I said yesterday I felt uneasy about sharing.' Toby was shouting now and people were staring, he didn't care. 'You've betrayed me Sir, and I don't ever want to see you again.' The teacher moved to console him, but Toby moved away. 'Stay away from me, just stay away.'

'But, Toby...'

Toby strode back to his friends; his fists clenched and face reddened.

'What's going on? What the hell did he say to fire you up like this?' Sophia stroked his arm, but he shrugged her away. 'Come on Toby, tell us what he said?'

'Yeah,' Nathan said, 'come on mate we're here to help.'

Bouncing on the spot like a prize-fighter, Toby took a few seconds to answer and when he did, it came with a hiss of words expelled through clenched teeth. 'He sent photos of my stuff to this professor Phillip Ryan. Now the professor wants my desk, the cabinet, the chair and everything. Somehow, he reckons it's all his.

Willy says he will go to any length to get it.' He shook his head as if to loosen his thoughts. 'The chalk faced old tool has dropped me in it big time.'

'So, what are you going to do?' Ben asked.

'Well I'm not doing English this afternoon, that's for sure,' Toby said, 'I'm heading for home now. And if anyone asks, say I cleared it with Willy. Come round after school? Reckon by then I'll need a bit of company.'

'Sure,' Sophia said, 'we'll all be there, won't we?'

Everyone agreed, and after they slapped palms, Toby slipped out of the school grounds and walked home.

CHAPTER TWELVE

'Steady Son,' Arthur said as Toby raced in the door, 'what's the hurry and why aren't you in school?'

Toby took a few deep breaths, grabbed a glass from the shelf and filling it with water from the fridge, felt his composure return. When the glass stood empty, he told Arthur everything.

'I'm going down the school.'

'Don't" Toby held out his hand, 'I don't think it'll make any difference now. I reckon Willy feels bad enough about it, besides he's not my immediate problem. How could this professor poonce even think he has a claim to something of mine?' Toby pressed his hands against the sink stretching the muscles along his spine, hoping it would relieve the tension he was feeling. 'It's like you said, it can't be for the money. I reckon there's a lot more to him that I don't know.' Toby looked around for the source of the draught he thought he was feeling. The room was closed. 'For a professor he just seems a bit... I don't know, creepy?'

'Toby, the desk is yours. Charlie'll have proof of purchase somewhere.' Arthur wrapped his arms around him holding the hug for over a minute, and patting his back as they broke away said, 'besides it would cost a power of coin to start court proceedings over its ownership. No, mate it's yours fair and square.' Arthur pushed back and looked directly at Toby. 'Now you go back to school, and I'll talk to Charlie.'

'I only have English classes for the rest of this morning, then lunch and sport after that, so I won't miss much. I'd sooner come to Charlie's.'

'Yeah okay, but only this time.'

Arthur insisted on taking the car and parked behind the shops. Locking it, he looked around to see if there was anyone loitering in the laneway. He kicked at a spoon and a syringe dropped in a doorway. 'That's despicable. Filthy, stinking, drug addicts, you'd reckon the council would make 'em clean up after themselves. If I ever catch you with any of that stuff, I'll kick your backside fair into tomorrow.'

'No need to worry Pop, I see enough of it at school. The kids who use, don't do the hard stuff, but weed spaces a few of them out.' Toby looked into his grandfather's eyes. 'I know what trouble is, Pop and I'm doing fine now thanks.'

'Good answer... Righto, now let's see if Charlie can help with our conundrum.'

'Bit more than a conundrum I reckon.'

'We'll see, but there's probably nothing to it.'

CHAPTER THIRTEEN

Holding the lunch that Pop had ordered, Toby pushed his way back into the shop and with no sign of the old men at the counter, he walked to the office where their voices were coming from.

'Yeah, well they're still all back there, mate. You and Toby are welcome to go through all of them anytime.'

Toby called out, but neither of them looked up from what it was they were doing. When he squeezed inside, he found them looking at a book perched on top of the filing cabinets.

'I'll pull them out later, see if Toby wants to have a sift through,' Arthur said, 'might help him to get his head around what was going on back then.'

Toby cleared his throat. 'Head around what?'

Charlie, looking up and thrusting the ledger at him, said, 'what've you got for us, Tobe?'

'Pie and chips. Food that built our nation, isn't it Pop?'

'Too right, none of that packaged cardboard stuff for us, was it Charlie? Arthur replied, 'always fish and chips in newspaper, or a pie and sauce,'

'Stuff that turned boys into men, and girls into young ladies,' Charlie said.

'What's with the book, Mr Rankin?' Toby said trying to brush decades of dust off the book.

'Toby, my young friend,' Charlie said, 'that is a Second-Hand Dealer's Register. We had to keep an itemised account of everything that came through our business. The police would call to check it at least once a month. More often at times, especially if there had been a spate of burglaries. My old Dad and his father before him kept excellent records. Somewhere in here, is what proves your desk came to us fair and square,' his greasy forefinger prodded the book, 'and when you've finished eating, we'll have a closer look at it.'

'So, you wrote everything down by hand?' Toby said stuffing a handful of chips into his mouth. The sooner he finished eating, the sooner he could start his search.

'In the old days, we had a couple of girls working as clerks, just keeping track of everything. Then there were the blokes who moved and stored the stock, and the sales guys, they went out canvassing for business. At times we had twenty people making a living here.' He turned away. His eyes moistened, and he looked at the street. 'They were the good old days Toby, good days indeed.'

'No computers like nowadays,' said Arthur, 'we even had to add up without using a calculator.'

As was their custom, they washed the pies and chips down with Charlie's favourite, sarsaparilla. Toby preferred an orange juice, but this was easier.

'Let's get this lot cleaned up. Your grandfather has found some of Franny Smith's old scrap books. She might have saved something about Shamus. You can look through them while me and Artie find the receipts for your desk.'

CHAPTER FOURTEEN

Toby had school tomorrow and although he wanted to avoid his teacher, he knew Mr Wyatt only wanted to help. He had encouraged and pushed him to extend himself, now it was time Toby let his anger slide. After all, Willy taught history too.

Toby wondered why Shamus had saved charcoal rubbings and about the numbers on them. Then there was the envelope, marked with Eagle's Talon in red pencil. It contained several photos and he liked one of a head-piece. He thought it may be a tiara, but would check with Sophia tomorrow. Then there were Charlie's scrapbooks. Toby used notes from a stick-it pad, to mark and date every reference to Shamus. Six books dated from 1924 to 1939 were stuffed with cuttings and all of them mentioned Shamus. Even in death, O'Toole created headlines and there was a lot of speculation about his death. The coroner ruled it was death by misadventure, but the press questioned his findings saying that Shamus had over administered his insulin. Toby too was suspicious, nothing in his research pointed to O'Toole being a diabetic.

Arthur knocked. 'Come on Tobe, it's late and you have school in the morning. I'm off to bed now and reckon you better do the same, eh?'

'Yeah, I'm about ready. I'll just put this picture in my bag and close up.' Toby yawned and rubbed his eyes.

'You might have to let this whole Shamus O'Toole thing settle for a bit. Let him rest in peace. He died nearly eighty years ago, so what do you think you can achieve by sifting through all of this now?'

Arthur's advice made sense, but Toby's desire to work it out was too strong. There was something about this whole thing that tugged at him, Willy was acting all strange, and then there was that damned professor too.

Arthur lingered at the door, and shifted his weight from one foot to the other. He scratched his chin. 'It's up to you Tobe, but remember, you have a big school year coming up, and I don't want to see you distracted.'

'Sure-thing Pop, another five minutes and I'll lock up.'

'Good lad, see you tomorrow.'

Arriving at school next morning, Toby saw Slasher limping past Mr Wyatt and heard the teacher call out. 'You okay, Daniel?'

He listened for Slasher's reply, but held back, most of the kids knew Slasher's home life was pretty tough and Toby knew what that was like. He'd had to leave to get away from it.

'Yes sir, why?' Slasher said.

'I thought you were limping that's all.'

'Rolled my ankle getting off the bus last night. I'll be right.'

'Just let me know if you're not?'

'Thanks, but I'm fine.' Slasher kept walking, head down. Toby knew what that felt like too.

It was time for a peace offering and he walked over to his teacher, 'Sir, about yesterday?'

'Toby, I should have asked first.'

'Maybe, but as Pop said, you were only trying to help. If this bloke, Professor Ryan, reckons he can prove he has some kinda claim to my desk, then he'll need to take it to court. Pop and Mr Ramsey found the receipt for it yesterday. Charlie called a lawyer friend who said to tell the Prof he could do his worst.'

'Toby, yes I was only trying to help, but it seems Phillip Ryan is still the bully I knew at uni. He's very driven; but even so, I can't believe he's reacted this way about a desk.'

'Sir, I need your help. I think Shamus was murdered, probably poisoned with insulin and I want to know why, and by who?'

'Whom,' the teacher said, 'I want to know by whom.'

'Yes sir, by whom.'

'You only have a few more days of this term left and I have a fair bit on my plate until then. However, if you make up a list of the things you'd like me to do, we can go from there, okay?'

'Just one more thing... well two really. Have you ever heard about something called the Ancient order of Pennyweights? And the other question is who, or what was the Eagles Talon?'

'Hmm, I think I've read something about a secret society called that, and the other one sounds like a jewel of some sort. Let me think about it for a while.'

'Thanks Sir, I'll see you in class.' Toby turned and sauntered toward his friends.

Jack, Ben, Nathan and Sophia looked up as Toby walked over to them. They looked like they had been talking and he thought he'd felt his ears burning.

'All right, are we?' Jack said.

'Yeah.' Toby pushed his friend's shoulder. 'Just had to blow out a few fuses, that's all.'

'You gave us a bit to wonder about,' Sophia held his shoulders and making sure she had eye contact, continued, 'and Toby, shooting through like that. I've never seen you so upset.'

Nathan added, 'You put the breeze up old Willy too. He was tearing all over the school asking if we knew where you were. I think he might have even driven past your place,'

'No harm done. I was browned off with him for sending copies of my stuff to this Professor Ryan bloke. Especially when he said he wouldn't. That creep—Ryan—reckons the desk is his. Well it's not, Pop and Charlie found a receipt for it yesterday. So Ryan can whistle, it's mine.' Toby thumped a fist into his other hand emphasising each word. 'Charlie's even lined up a lawyer.'

'You have been busy.' Sophia said.

'But I still need help, are you in?'

'Yep.' Jack said.

'With bells on.' Sophia agreed.

Nathan was caught up in the excitement agreed, saying, 'me too.'

Ben just nodded.

'We'd better go in, but at recess I've found something to show you, but not a word to anyone though, understand?'

The friends tip touched their right hands to signal agreement.

CHAPTER FIFTEEN

The recess signal had barely started when Toby and his friends sprinted to their favourite meeting place. The contents of a large yellow envelope slid out and Toby unfolded one of the charcoal rubbings from Shamus's files. He took out the old green journal and opened it to where the closest index number he had found corresponded.

'What do you make of this?' he said.

'Well, see the date on the page?' Sophia pointed to a spot in the open journal. 'The numbers don't correspond unless you reverse them, now look at the charcoal rubbing. If you reverse its number, they're the same. It makes this rubbing correspond to the date in the journal. Now the question is, what does the rubbing tell us?'

'That other number in the journal, they're like numbers in a street directory. Oh, what do you call it?' There was frustration in Ben's voice. 'A map reference, that's it a map reference.'

'What-cha all got there, bookworms?' Slasher stood above them. He pocketed his phone quickly.

'Rack off Sabo.' Toby was on his feet, a hand against Slasher's chest, pushing him back. 'This has nothing to do with you.'

'Or what, you'll have your girlfriend fight your battles for you?'

'I can do you.'

'That day can't come soon enough for me, Farrier, then we'll see if your words stack up.' Slasher said and turned away. 'You can jam your damn book up your nose for all I care.'

'What's with him?' Sophia said. 'He just won't leave us alone. Did you see what he was doing with his phone? Was he taking photos?'

'Don't let him get to you,' Toby said. 'He's all noise.'

The day dragged, maths followed by science and another round of maths coupled with social studies. Toby tried to stop his thoughts wandering to the journal. Could Sophia be right, and why did Shamus code everything? Ben seemed to be just as distracted. He was asked a question two times in a row, but he didn't know what was being talked about. The teacher tossed a piece of chalk in Nathan's direction more than once, telling him to wipe the smirk off his face. Toby took a look at him and he was grinning his head off; maybe he was thinking about the mystery of the journal too. Sophia was the only one of their group who seemed to be concentrating today.

As they walked toward the school gate, she said, 'I found that social studies lesson interesting, Toby. Didn't you?'

'Couldn't get into it at all. All I can think about is Shamus and his coded clues,' Toby said. 'It's doing my head in.'

'Yeah, but did you hear the teacher describing things about the Global Finance Crisis a couple of years back, and how it's affecting people now. And will do for years to come.'

'Sure, but did I get what she meant. No.'

'Well if you remember, she talked about the lead up to the GFC and how money was lent to people who really had no way of making their repayments. In the end, a lot of people went broke.'

'Yeah, Pop and Charlie go on about it all the time, it bores me silly.'

'Think about it though? The same thing was happening in Shamus's time. I think he must have found something important and needed to hide whatever it was.'

'So you reckon someone killed him to keep him quiet?'

'It's a pretty big leap from a financial collapse to murder, Toby.'

'Yeah, well I know there's something fishy about all of this.'

'I've been giving some thought to those rubbings too. I think I have seen markings like those on gravestones. You know the type usually carved out of marble or granite. Could the references be the location of the graves?'

'Well I suppose it's possible, but why be so cryptic?' said Toby.

'I don't know, anyway Mum's here now. I'll come around about five, but I can only stay for an hour. We'll talk more about it then.'

'Do you know if the others are coming?'

'I think so, but don't know what time.

'Later,' Toby said and pushed on toward home.

'Yeah, later then.'

CHAPTER SIXTEEN

Toby heard someone coming from behind. The footsteps were closer now, more than two or three people and closing fast. He turned to see how far back they were; the Slater gang were about fifty metres back. If he sprinted, he might get home before they caught him. He saw Slasher waiting a couple of houses from his gate. He'd walked into an ambush. Alone, Toby could handle Slash, but the whole gang was a different matter. Toby's heart responded to adrenalin, and wondered if he should surrender, but his nature wouldn't allow it. They were all around him now and fleeing was no longer an option. Negotiation the only option.

'Move Sabo, let me pass… please.' the last word dragging through gritted teeth

'Not gunna happen bookworm, you've got something we want.' Slasher waved a box cutter under Toby's nose. No one else in the gang spoke.

'What? I have nothing you could want.'

'Don't be an idiot,' he took a box cutter from his pocket and extended the blade. 'I want that old book you and Soph were gawping at this morning.'

'Why? What's so important that would make you yobs try to grab it?' Toby looked at each of them in the circle and said, 'who's put you up to it?'

Slasher held his other hand out and said, 'Look, make it easy on yourself, just hand it over and you won't get hurt.'

'Bull, someone's put you up to it.' Toby slapped Slasher's hand away and pushed his chest. 'Tell me I'm wrong?'

'Easy Twerp, you're wrong.' Slasher withdrew the blade, slipped the cutter back into his pocket and turned away. 'Cops boys.'

In an instant the gang dissipated, all sauntering off in different directions.

Slasher remained. 'I'm gunna have that book Farrier, even if I have to cut you or your girlfriend to get it.'

A police van stopped alongside them. 'Everything under control here?' Toby thought the officer looked familiar. 'What are your names, boys?' He opened the door and walked over to them.

'Toby Farrier, Sir.'

'Daniel Sir, Daniel Sabo.'

'Live around here, do you?'

Toby said, 'Yeah, I'm a few houses further up the street.'

'And I'm a couple of blocks away.'

The constable who rode in the passenger seat was standing with them now. 'What about your mates, why did they run?' She looked into Slasher's eyes. 'The truth now. You know I'm not too pleased when I learn later that people have been less than honest with me.'

'Well, they had to get their homework done. We've got a big assignment due for tomorrow's English lesson, and we were asking if Toby could help with it.'

'Yeah, and what did Toby say?'

'Turned us down, has too much other work to do. Can't help this time, but I'm sure he'll help us out before the lesson.'

'Toby,' she asked, 'is that what really happened?'

Toby nodded. 'I don't have the time.'

The first constable said, 'Okay, Daniel, you can get on your way now. And lose the box cutter. You're lucky Toby didn't give you up.'

The female cop peered at Slasher. 'I've seen you before, haven't I?'

'Maybe, I run a few errands for a couple of shop keepers from time to time,' Slasher said.

'On your way then, and I don't want to see you or your mates for the rest of the week.'

Slasher sauntered off.

The first constable turned and looking Toby up and down, said. 'Toby Farrier, there was a wild kid of that name in Kyneton when I lived there. Gave his parents hell.' The officer stared at him and Toby shifted his feet. 'Sent him to live with his grandad. That be you, Toby?'

'Yes Sir.'

'See much of your olds, these days?' His eyes looked at Toby intensely.

'I haven't seen them since I left. They cut me out of their lives,' Toby said and looked away; he could feel sadness drive tears into his eyes. He did miss the full family experience. He often thought about his dad and wondered would he ever be welcomed back. 'Maybe one day...' he couldn't finish the sentence.

The female officer asked, 'Slasher bother you much?'

'He didn't say his name was Slasher.'

'No, but we know the family. The poor kid doesn't have much of a chance.'

'I can handle him on his own, but I'm glad you showed up when you did.' Toby started to relax and did the thing he promised himself he'd never do. 'Do you see them ever, you know, my dad and the girls?' He looked at the policeman.

'Yeah, saw your dad at the supermarket last time I was home.' The officer said.

'Was he good?'

'Yeah, the kids were with him, real happy family. Want me to say hello next time I'm home?'

'Nah, better not, don't want to complicate things,' Toby said.

'Here's my card,' the policeman said. 'if you want me to, I'll say hello.'

Toby stared at the policeman's name on the card, Constable John Evans. Then said, 'thanks, but I've got heaps of chores to do, so now I'd better get home.'

CHAPTER SEVENTEEN

Arthur was standing at the front gate when Toby walked up to it. 'What'd the coppers want?' he said. 'Was that bloody Sabo kid bothering you again?'

'Yeah, he wanted Shamus's journal, was trying to grab it when the cops pulled up.'

'I heard the siren whip and came out for a look.'

'Not like you, Pop? You're always telling me not to worry about what's going on in the street,' Toby laughed, 'but thanks for looking out for me.'

'Better get inside and get your homework outta the way before you mess around with that book again.'

'I will, Pops.' Toby rolled his eyes, mocking his grandfather. 'You know I will.'

'On ya bike son. I'm off to check on Charlie, back in about an hour.'

'My mates are coming around later, that okay with you, Pop?'

'Just get that homework done first.'

His homework complete, Toby waited for Sophia and the others to arrive. He'd started to list the events O'Toole had highlighted in the diary. Shamus was tracking something and every so often he underlined a letter of a word with red ink. It had to be code or something just as important, but what?

The back door banged open and Arthur came in with Sophia trailing behind him. 'Look who I found waiting at the gate.' Arthur had a large parcel under his arm, the aroma of hot fish and chips wafted around him. 'Charlie's coming with pizza and Ben and Nathan will be here soon too. We have plenty of soft drink in the fridge.' The package thudded into the centre of the table. 'Get some lemons from the tree, there's a good lad.' Arthur's voice had a happy urgency about it. He skipped a little dance, grabbed glasses from the sideboard and put them on the table. As Sophia stood to help him, he took her hand and waltzed her around the room.

'You're a happy man tonight, Mr Farrier.' Sophia giggled.

'We have news, good news, but not until everyone is here.'

'What kind of news?' Toby asked.

'Wait until everyone's here.' Arthur's forefinger tapped his nose. 'Then I'll let the cat outa the bag.'

The back door squeaked open. 'Ya there Artie?' Charlie had loaded Ben and Nathan with pizza. 'Come on boys, put the boxes on the bench. Fingers or plates tonight, mate?'

'What about it, kids?' Arthur said, hoping for fingers.

Everyone agreed fingers would be fine. Toby and Ben pushed the table back against the wall and put the chairs into a semi-circle, allowing easy access to the food.

'Smells alright.' Nathan said. 'What's the go, Mr Farrier? Why the celebration and why on a school night. It's a bit out of character, even for Toby?'

'Well, me and Charlie here, have a bit of news, and I reckon Toby is going to be chuffed when he hears it. But we're not saying anything until your folks get here,' Arthur winked at him, 'make you wait for a while, just a bit of a tease, mate.'

'Is it about Shamus?' Toby asked. 'What have you found?'

'No. Listen, Tobe, we'll get tea over and the kitchen cleared away, first. Okay?'

Toby strained to hear for cars stopping in the street. Even the pizza seemed to crunch louder tonight. The aroma of cheese melted over ham. The salt of the chips, and lemon on the fish couldn't distract him. He swished a mouth full of coke from his can, as he tried to quench the fire from a chip too hot for his mouth. Nothing could ease his eagerness to know what secret this pair of senior citizens shared. Why couldn't they just tell him? Ben and Nathan were talking about the holidays and what they'd planned to do. He could see Sophia's lips moving, but he didn't understand what she was telling his grandfather, and Charlie tried without success to cut pizza with a fork.

'For pity's sake man, pick it up in your fingers. We don't stand on ceremony here.' Arthur laughed, and tossing him a knife from the drawer, added. 'Here you go mate, take to it with that.'

Toby ushered his friend's folks through the back door until the small kitchen was bursting at the seams.

CHAPTER EIGHTEEN

Arthur ushered everyone out into the garden. He rattled the string of the wind chime. 'I know this is a week night and you've got work or school tomorrow, so I'll be quick. Me and Charlie wanted to share our news with our friends first.' He looked across to his old friend and said. 'You'd better tell 'em mate.'

'Well, as you know, me and Artie have been putting a system-sevens entry into TattsLotto every week for years.' A chuckle went through the listeners. 'Yeah, yeah, I know things don't change much and yes, we do play the same numbers all the time. Well this week was a jackpot draw, and blow me down, our numbers came up.'

Jack and Nathan let out whoops and high fived.

'Settle down, we didn't get the big prize, but we got enough to make life a bit easier for Artie and me.'

'How much?' Questions like this escaping from Ben's mouth were regular and annoying.

'Enough,' Arthur said. 'Now that Toby has his own study, I'll be able to get him a few things. A new computer, a better mobile phone and some other furniture. I'd even suggest a new desk, but I don't think he'd want it.' He raised his eyebrows and another chuckle erupted.

Sophia said. 'Is that why you've called us all here tonight, Mr Farrier?'

Charlie answered her. 'That's part of it. You see Artie has a favour to ask, we've wanted to see Gallipoli and the pyramids since we were kids, and this little windfall makes it possible. It's just...'

Toby turned to his grandfather. 'It's just that you have me to worry about isn't it, Pop.' He felt tears start to come. 'What do you do with a fifteen-year-old kid,' his eyes searched his grandfather's face, 'I'm a bit of a drag if you want to go away, aren't I?'

'Tobe, there's no way I'd ever consider you a drag, and having you to think about, well yeah, that's some of it, but there's another thing as well.'

'Another thing?' Toby's mind raced. 'What other thing?'

'Well I reckon I could get you into a boarding school while we're away, but Charlie reckons you'd be better off in your own home. And...' he looked around the adult's faces, 'if these good people can check up on you from time to time, it'll be okay with me.' Toby felt Arthur slip an arm around him. 'Now I don't want you running all over Melbourne trying to get to the bottom of O'Toole's mystery while we're away. So, you'd better work it out, and soon.'

'Anything we can do to help, Artie?' Nathan's dad said, 'I work in the city most days, but I can spare a bit of time on the weekends and my office has a good research team,'

'We only live a few houses down the street so I can help him with his washing and the housework.' Sophia's mum offered.

'Thanks, but Toby's okay with chores, but an occasional check to see he's keeping the place tidy and if you follow up on his homework, it'd settle my mind while we're away.'

Arthur smiled at his friends. 'Okay with you, Toby?' he said and gave him a gentle shake.

'Yeah, good, better than I expected.' Toby was smiling. When he first moved to Brunswick, trust was hard to earn. 'You mean it? I can live here on my own and you'll trust me to go to school and all while you're away?'

'Yep, and I'm gunna get me one of those iBody thingos so I can sky... Oh, what do they call it, you know when you can see each other during a phone call?'

'Skype, and I think you mean iPad, Mr Farrier. You will skype Toby on your new iPad.' Sophia smirked. 'Don't worry, Mr Farrier we can help get you started, after all, Dad has a place that sells this stuff. Right, Dad?'

Using his best English Sophia's father agreed. 'We'll get you sorted Artie, just call in to the shop when you can?'

'Mate's rates, Ahn?'

'Mate's rates, Artie.'

Toby felt Nathan's dad lock eyes with him. 'Tell you what, Tobe. Our facility does research for television programmes, film projects and government agencies. Why don't I get a couple of researchers to look into Melbourne's upper crust and any possible links to the crime gangs of the era? I can write it off to a film project I'm ready to produce. If anything interesting comes across my desk, I'll let you know.'

Nathan had said his father was an executive in the city and had his own company, but Toby had never been that interested. He was just happy to know Nathan was his friend.

'Thanks, but no thanks, I couldn't afford to pay you.'

'Don't worry, Toby, this is on me, who knows, you might have a story to sell when this is all done.'

Through the evening the group talked and made plans. Saturday Toby would check out the State Library.

CHAPTER NINETEEN

Sophia's dad looked at the spreadsheet she and Toby were working on.

His accent hinted Vietnamese roots and Toby liked the way Ahn's 'r's sounded like 'w's. 'I think we can crack this one with a bit of work. Soph, if you double check all of your entries and, Toby, see this here?' He pointed to the red pencil marks underlining the letters in the words. 'Look at the way each one is different, a bump here and a scroll there. I think your mister Shamus was being very clever, he has hidden a secret in these words, one only he can read. If you separate each letter and list them with the same squiggles, I think you'll work it out. Remember it's a diary, so work page by page, week by week, month by...'

'Yeah, Dad we get it.'

'You do?' Ben scratched his head. Nathan peered over his shoulder.

'Well, we'd better leave you to it and take our boy home. I'll bet he's still got homework left to do,' Ben's dad said.

'Yeah us too, I've got an early start tomorrow.' Nathan's mother started putting chairs away.

Arthur came in from seeing Charlie off. Toby was putting the last of things away in the kitchen. 'Wow Pop, you blokes had a win, how good's that?' Toby was happy for them and proud he'd earned his grandfather's trust. 'So I'll stay here, by myself and no adult supervision?'

'You'll have supervision alright, but I'm sure I can trust you. You'll just have to treat the place the same as if I were here, that's all, and if you don't, well I'll never trust you again. You know that.'

'It'll be okay. I promise.'

'Deal then?'

'Deal.'

Arthur was about to lock up when he saw a police car cruise into the driveway. 'Toby, your friend from this arvo has just pulled up.'

'Who?'

'The copper, looks like the same one.' Arthur pushed a couple of chairs into the table and went to the door to meet him.

'Mr Farrier, I'm Constable John Evans. Is Toby home?'

'John Evans from Kyneton?'

'Yeah that's right. My sister went to school with Darren's wife.'

Toby was at Arthur's shoulder and said. 'So you knew my mum?' He felt heartened by the connection, but wondered what the policeman could want at this time of night.

'Young Danny Sabo was bashed by his uncle tonight and we suspect his father helped. Toby, I just wanted to know if the fact that he pulled a box cutter on you might have had anything to do with it.'

'I don't think so,' Toby ran his fingers through his hair and slumped against the wall. If he'd given Slash the book maybe he'd have been okay, he pushed the thought from his mind. Besides, the constable said it was his uncle who did the bashing. 'I do know he's got a new mobile phone. So apart from that and the fact that he's on my back to give him a book I found last week, I can't see how what happened today would have anything to do with it.'

Arthur balled his fists. 'Pulled a box cutter on you, did he? I'd have given him what for if I'd seen that.'

'It's okay, Pop. But about Slash, is he okay?'

'He's not good and I don't think you'll see him at school until after the holidays. Let me know if any of his cronies give you any trouble, yeah?' John said.

'I'll be right. Without Slash, they're weak-as... but thanks anyway.'

'Now, this book you found,' The policeman asked. 'Why would he want that?'

'You know what kids are like,' Arthur said, 'if they know you have something they don't, and you won't tell them what it is. Well, curiosity gets the better of them and they just hafta have it. And, I'll bet that's what's going on here.'

'You're probably right.'

Toby and his grandfather walked the policeman out.

CHAPTER TWENTY

For Toby, the next few days disappeared under a mix of lessons and his research into Shamus O'Toole. Constable Evans' visit had unsettled him and something he never thought would bother him, niggled away in his mind. Slasher might be a jumped-up prawn, but he didn't deserve a belting by his uncle. Toby thought back to his own situation as a kid. Sure, he had his share of discipline, but his dad never gave him more than a slap, and there must have been times when his behaviour deserved it. No, Arthur taking him in was something special, but he'd never felt unsafe at home with his dad.

'Pop, you might reckon I'm weird, but I reckon I'd like to go and see how Slash is doing.'

'Geez, Tobe, are you soft in the head, Son? I mean the kid pulled a knife on you.'

'Yeah, but it didn't come to anything, did it?' Toby answered, 'and you've always taught me to face my fears, to meet every challenge head on. Well I think it's time to perhaps to get over our differences. Who knows, we could end up being mates.' The smirk on Toby's face betrayed his words. He just wanted to break the animosity between them.

'Good grief, Toby are you mad? If you're gunna do this, I'll pave the way a bit, just let me call his Mum first.'

'You know, Mrs Sabo?'

'Yeah, we see each other about. She should have left that good-for-nothing years ago. She and young

Danny would have been a lot better off if she'd kicked him out when he first belted her.'

'But how?'

'It's a long time ago, but your Nan gave her comfort off and on.'

'Are you gunna tell me more?'

'Nope, it's a lifetime ago now, and Nan wouldn't want to have it brought up anyway.'

'Come on, Pop?'

'No Toby. And that's an end to it.'

Arthur didn't raise his voice often and seeing tears build in his eyes, Toby knew Nan was a subject best left alone. Pop was as tough as nails and would fight to protect his family, but tonight his grandfather looked vulnerable, so Toby backed off.

It was safer without Slash and his band of thugs terrorising the schoolyard. Freckles had assumed the position of top dog in the gang, but it wasn't the same. Kids just laughed at him, and the Slater Street Gang lost most of its cred. Toby knew why Slasher was missing school but kept it to himself.

'You've been a bit of a recluse Tobe, is everything alright?' Sophia asked, 'we saw the police car at your house after we left last night. Are you hiding something from us?' She slapped her hand over her mouth, 'oh no, you've done something to that Sabo creep, that's it, isn't it?'

'I haven't seen Slash. I'm just wondering how I'll go with Pop and Charlie gone for a couple of months, that's all.'

'Well you'd tell me if there was something wrong, wouldn't you? After all I'm practically your girlfriend.'

Toby turned to face her. He liked Sophia, but what did he know about girls. He thought they were just mates and now she says something like this. What could he say without hurting her feelings?

'Your face Farrier, it was priceless.' Sophia was jumping around and giggling. 'I got you good Toby. Now lose the gloomy mood before I tell all the girls in school, we're an item.'

'Sorry, I'll try a bit harder, okay?' He forced a smile and although he knew it wasn't convincing, he needed to lift his spirits.

'Good,' she said.

Toby knocked on the open door to Slasher's ward, but not before listening to the voice he recognised as Constable Evans who was out of uniform, and a woman who he assumed was Mrs Sabo. Their talking stopped and both looked up. Slasher's mother put something he took to be the policeman's business card in her pocket.

Toby wondered if he'd made a mistake coming here. 'Er... Pop said he'd let you know that I might drop in, is it okay?'

Mrs Sabo looked sad. Her face carried the lines of a woman twice her age. She wore no makeup and her hair was beginning to grey. She would have been pretty when she was young, he thought, and even though she was sitting, she still owned a fine figure. She smiled at him, there was no mistaking this was Slasher's mum, the twinkle in her eye and the edges of her mouth curled in the same way his did.

'Come in, Toby, Artie wouldn't have known how to find me, but that doesn't matter now. Why did you come? I know you and Danny are like oil and water.'

John stood and shook Toby's hand. With a wave, he offered his chair.

'I'm fine thanks,' Toby said, 'happy to stand.' He looked at Slasher. How vulnerable he looked. A tube carrying a solution, led up to a bag filled with the same coffee coloured liquid. High above the bed it hung from a chrome stand. The tube disappeared into Slasher's nose. Toby swallowed hard, trying to keep his own gastric juices down. In the corner of the ward, a set of bellows rose and fell rhythmically, Danny's chest moved in time to its action. Toby's eyes traced its hose and stared, they had taped it to Slasher's mouth and he assumed the tube plunged deep into his chest cavity. More wires of different colours snaked from under the crisp white sheet to a monitor, where even more coloured lines darted in random patterns across the screen. His head felt light, the room swirled and he could hear Mrs Sabo say.

'You better grab him mate, he's going to pass out,'

In one motion John stood, put his hands on Toby's shoulders and spun him into the chair.

When Toby opened his eyes he saw Slasher's mum holding a cup of water to his lips.

'Come on Toby, take a sip. You just fainted,' she said. 'It looks worse than it is. Danny's going to be alright.'

He felt comfort in her words and as she came into focus, Toby realised this was the first time in years he'd had any kind of motherly contact. This was something Slash had, that he didn't.

'I'm sorry, Mrs Sabo, I shouldn't have come.'

'Nonsense, you'll be right. You're a good kid Toby, and it takes guts just to come and visit an enemy. Which now makes me ask why you'd want to come?'

'I dunno, I guess in some ways we're not that different. I know I'm lucky I have Pop looking out for me and my own Dad, although he didn't want me, I understand, I suppose. Anyway, he never belted me either. I guess I just wanted Slash, I mean Danny, to...'

'He'll be like this for a few days, but when the doctors wake him up I'll tell him you dropped in.' She stretched her arm around his shoulders and with a gentle squeeze said, 'You're a good kid, mate and I'm sure if your dad had seen you just now, he'd think so too.'

Toby looked over to the policeman who was watching them with a curious look on his face.

Evans smiled at him. 'Well I'd better go, is there anything I can do for you, Helen?'

'No thanks, I've been looking after stuff on my own for a long time now, I reckon I'll manage for a few more days.'

'Well if you do need an errand run, or anything, you call me okay.' He reached out to shake her hand. 'My private number is on the back of the card.' He looked at Toby. 'Can I give you a lift home mate, or do you want to stay here for a bit?'

'Thanks, a lift'll be good.' Toby was eager to leave his embarrassment about fainting behind, and hoped Mrs Sabo would keep it to herself. 'I'm sorry about earlier. Tell Danny I'll come back when he's a bit more...'

'Awake?' Helen Sabo smiled.

'Yeah, awake sounds good.' Toby shook her hand, it was soft and warm, just the way a mother's should be. Without thinking, he leaned in and kissed her on the cheek. 'See-ya.'

CHAPTER TWENTY-ONE

The copper was quiet as he drove Toby home. A few times he opened his mouth as though to say something, but then stopped himself. Toby wound down the window and welcomed the fresh air.

'Fumes got to you a bit in there, eh?' Evans said as he turned into Sydney Road.

'Thanks for this, beats taking the tram. I don't know what happened, I just went all woozy.'

'Never seen anyone all hooked up like that before? I was the same my first time. They say it gets easier, but I'm not sure. I think you just learn to cover things up. I know I do.'

'I dunno,' Toby said. 'all those tubes and wires, the monitors, he looked so weak and helpless. I almost wanted him to spring up and abuse me. You know, just so I knew he was alive.'

'So, why did you go?'

'I knew none of his gang'd front. They're all tough and that when Slash is dragging them along, but weak as...' he wanted to swear but thought better of it, 'on their own. He hasn't got any real mates and I dunno, I guess I wanted to let him know he's not on his own.' The words swelled in Toby's throat and he took his time enunciating them. 'I s'pose you think I'm a bit weak too.'

'Not at all,' John said, 'it takes guts to do what you did tonight. I'm not sure if I'd have done it at your age.' John focussed on the road ahead then pointed to the fast food sign and said. 'I wouldn't mind a sundae, how about it?'

'Sounds good.' Toby narrowed his eyes and turned to the policeman as the car stopped. 'When are you going to Kyneton again?'

'Oh, I don't know, in a couple of weeks probably, why?'

'It's just that I've been thinking about what you said and, yeah, I'd like you to say hello to Dad for me.'

'Is that it, I told you I'd be happy to.' John winked at him. 'Come on let's get an icecream inside you.'

'And, one other favour.'

'Another favour, yeah sure, but I've got a couple of things I want to ask you too.'

'I thought you might.' Toby smiled. 'Otherwise we'd be home by now.'

They sat on stools with their elbows resting on the bench that ran along the restaurant's front windows that overlooked Sydney Road. The icecream tasted good and they said nothing to each other while watching the traffic thin out.

The policeman wiped his hands and turning to face Toby asked. 'What was the other thing you wanted to ask me?'

'Nah, you go first. I reckon you're gunna ask me about Slash and if I know why his dad did what he did.' Toby turned and smiled. 'Is that it?'

'Kind of, I wondered about his mobile phone. Do you know how long he has had it?'

'Can't be sure. He had it at school last week. He didn't have it before that. He was hanging around me, Soph and the guys the other day, making out he was spying on us with it. I think he might have taken photos or something. I told him to shove off. He gave me a mouthful and went back to his mates.'

'Yeah, but what were you doing at the time?'

'Not much that'd interest him, just looking through an old book I found in the desk that I got from Charlie, I mean Mr Ramsey. Why?'

'Not sure, but something's not right and I have a suspicion it's to do with his phone.' John frowned. 'Come on, Arthur will be wondering where you are.' John pulled the door open and they stepped into the evening. It was cooler now and the rumble of the city had dropped a bit. 'What did you want to ask me?'

'You said your sister went to school with my mum, I wondered if you'd ask her if I could write, or call her, or something. I never knew my real mum and I'd like to talk to someone who did. You probably think I'm being a bit soppy?'

'Nope, I'll give Sis a call, and let you know. Might take a few days though.'

'Ta, I appreciate it, but not a word to Pop until I've talked to him, alright?'

'It's a deal.' John parked opposite Arthur's home.

'Thanks for the ride.' Toby stepped out and held the car door open for a moment. A car at the end of the block caught his attention. It looked out of place here.

'Say hello to Arthur for me.'

'Sure,' Toby said and keeping his eyes on the Audi coupe, dodged a car coming up the street. Still looking at the silver car, he paused at the gate before slipping around to the back door of the house. Inside he listened, straining to hear John's car moving off slowly; maybe he too had slowed to look at that. That's what cops did. Toby shook off any strange feelings. If it was someone dodgy, the police would check it out.

Arthur didn't look up when Toby came into the room. 'G'day, Tobe, I'm sorry I couldn't get hold of Mrs Sabo, I don't think she's been home. I tried to phone, but it just rang out.'

'Yeah, no worries, Pop. She was cool. That copper, John, was there too. I didn't think seeing Slash would stir me up so much.' Toby didn't want to break down in front of his grandfather, but he felt hot in the pit of his stomach. 'Pop, he's so sick, pipes and tubes coming out of him everywhere, and Mrs Sabo says it'll be a while before they wake him up.'

'So, do you feel better about seeing him?'

'I dunno? I fainted when I saw him. I couldn't believe it and she, Mrs Sabo well she, she made me feel better.'

'Told you she was a good-un,' Arthur said. 'Made you wonder what it's like to have a mum to watch out for you, eh?'

'Something like that. Even with him all hooked up to those wires and stuff, I couldn't help feeling a bit envious. In amongst all of his problems, he still has his mum.'

'Tobe, I don't know what to say, I can only do what I do, Son.'

'I know, Pops, I just miss her sometimes.'

'You probably miss 'em all. I'll try your dad again, before me and Charlie head overseas. See if they'll agree to see us before I go.'

'I'm fine, Pop, really.'

'Okay, we'll talk about it later, how about some dinner and then you can tell me about the rest of your day.'

CHAPTER TWENTY-TWO

Tomorrow being the first day of the holidays, Toby's friends had reneged, saying they had other commitments. He was disappointed they couldn't go to the library with him, but reasoned he'd discover more on his own. Charlie and Arthur had a trip to plan, and a note on the fridge told Toby he'd be on his own tonight. He'd stayed on his own before, but tonight he felt more alone than he could remember. Fridays had always been fun, but tonight all he wanted to do was cry. Worse still, he didn't know where these feelings were coming from.

He woke to Arthur prising the fountain pen from his hand and shaking him.

'Come on Tobe, we'd better get you into bed.'

Toby shuffled with Arthur's support from his desk to his bed.

'Kick your shoes off Tobe and I'll cover you with the bedspread for tonight.' Arthur bent over and kissed his cheek, before saying, 'goodnight son, I love you mate.'

In the morning, Toby found Arthur in the shed tinkering with the lawnmower. 'What are you doing, Pop?'

'The old girl needs a service and some new blades. You okay? You hardly woke up when I helped you into bed?'

'I couldn't make sense of some stuff that's all. I dropped off I suppose.'

'You still going into town today? I can come too if you want.'

'Nah, I'll be right, I'd have liked the others to come, but it's okay.'

'Did what's-his-name's dad find anything to help break the code?'

'Nah, I guess it's not as important to them, and they've all got other family stuff to do this week.'

'Feeling a bit left out, eh?'

'A bit.' Toby turned away and said, 'If you like, I'll cut the lawns after breakfast tomorrow.'

'You're on, she'll go like a beauty too, new blades and all, won't take you long.'

'I'll go into the library today, okay?'

'You'll be careful?'

'Yes, Pop, and I might swing by the hospital again on the way home too.' Toby looked down at his feet. 'Okay with that?'

'I'm beggared if I'll ever understand why? but yeah, it's fine. You're a good kid, and I'm proud of...' Arthur looked away.

'I'll just grab some stuff and walk down to Sydney Road to catch the tram.'

'Give me ten minutes and I'll knock up a sandwich for you.'

Toby shoved a green covered ledger that had once served Shamus as a note book, and his lunch into a backpack. He grabbed the pages photocopied from the journal and his list of the squiggles Shamus had scrawled under his notes.

'Here's an apple and some biscuits, put them in too. Now, you've got your Myki card?' Arthur asked.

'Yeah.' Toby stuffed the pages and his lunch in with the ledger.

'Mobile phone?'

'Nope, won't need it, besides the battery's flat. I'll charge it tonight.'

'Well take care and get home before tea, okay?' Arthur pressed a ten dollar note into Toby's hand. 'Just in case you need something.'

'Pop, I have cash.'

'Shush, and I only have one grandson, take it.'

'Thanks.'

'Now Charlie and I are going out again tonight, you be alright on your own again. I'll leave dinner in the fridge, okay?'

'Yeah Pops, I'll be fine. Enjoy your night out, have you old fellas hooked with a couple of mature minded women?'

'Listen to you, mature minded women, where do you kids get this stuff?'

'I read the paper Pops, I read everything,' Toby's index finger touched the side of his nose, 'your secret's safe with me, old man.'

Feeling the hair on his neck prickle and a shiver go through him, Toby turned around, but nothing looked out of place. However, he saw a sports car at the end of the street and, convinced it was the same one as the other day when John dropped him home, shivered again. It wasn't unusual to have strangers parking there, as the rental units around the corner had no visitor parking. However, this car made him uncomfortable. Was someone watching him, or was he imagining stuff? It had to be his imagination. He'd put it out of his mind, get on the tram, go to the library and discover everything he could about Shamus.

Surrounded by oak panelling and books. Toby opened the ledger and sorted through his notes from last night. Nothing made sense anymore and a veil of confusion settled in his mind. Thoughts of his family in Kyneton flashed in his memory and he smiled. Then the bad memories flowed; he'd been angry, lonely and worthless. It startled him. He knew everything he'd planned for today could wait until he was ready. Damn Mrs Sabo, if she hadn't been so nice, he wouldn't have missed his mother's touch.

'Sorry Shamus, you'll have to wait.' Toby didn't know why he was apologising to someone who'd been dead for years. Or why he needed to see Slasher. He only knew he couldn't handle feeling alone today. His backpack caught on the chair as he slung it over his shoulder, the clatter causing a group of girls to giggle and twitter. He felt even more insignificant and couldn't wait to leave. Toby, one hand clinging to the shoulder strap and the other clutching the ledger, rushed out to wait for the tram.

Bony fingers whipped across his hand, Toby hearing the slap before feeling its sting. As he looked up at the man who had hit him, the book fell from his grip. The stranger bending, his hand reaching for it, but Toby's determination was grater and he snatched the ledger from the pavement. Running across the front of an oncoming tram and looking over his shoulder, he saw the stranger still straightening his back as he put the tram between the attacker and himself. Why would someone want this book, and how would they know he'd be here? It wasn't part of his routine to be waiting for this tram. He shivered and for the second time today, he felt the hair on his neck prick. The look in the stranger's eyes frightened him. Toby's mind raced, he ran through the narrow laneways of Melbourne. He needed somewhere safe.

Clutching his chest and swallowing hard he tasted bile in his mouth. Still running he fought faintness. He flung himself onto the north bound tram. It took a moment to steady himself, gasping deep breaths the incoming air burnt his lungs. Toby looked back, hoping he had lost his pursuer.

Getting off the tram again become a priority, the old geezer might have seen him. Toby tried to slow his mind and remember what had happened. He looked at the welts on the back of his hand. They changed to a deeper red as he studied them and he wondered if the stinging would ever stop. Without thinking he rubbed his hand, trying to assure himself the skin was still there.

The next stop was outside the Royal Melbourne Hospital. He could lose himself there.

CHAPTER TWENTY-THREE

The smell of brewing coffee wafted around the cafeteria, Toby found a spot in the back and started sketching the guy who slapped him. Here he could go unnoticed long enough to make some notes, only going home when he felt it was safe.

The tomato sauce had seeped into the bread of his sandwich, he tasted the Strasburg sausage and he smiled, it was his favourite filling. 'Yeah, this'll do,' he said to no one in particular. The pulse of the hospital, combined with the food, eased his mind, and Toby began to feel his confidence return.

He tried again to make sense of his notes, but it might well have been alphabet soup. His thoughts drifted to Slasher, why did he keep haunting him? Hell, he didn't even like the bloke and didn't deserve a visit, but Toby knew he wouldn't rest if he walked away without saying hello to Mrs Sabo.

He would stick his head in the door, say hello and be out of there. Yeah, that's the plan, he thought, and waited for the lift doors to open. Staring at nothing in particular, passengers exited in a mass of grey movement. Toby stepped in and shuffled to the back, questioning the sense of it. Something stirred his memory, faint at first, it rolled in his mind tumbling in and out of his childhood. That was it, the smell. It struggled its way through the normal scent of a lift that conveyed smokers, diners, and workers through the caverns of the building. This was feminine and familiar, yet hard to place. The doors opened and it was gone. He knocked on the opening to Slasher's ward and stuck his head in.

'Rack off Farrier. I don't need to see you gloating over my problems.'

'Nice to see you too, turnip.' Toby couldn't hide the sneer in his response. Slasher always knew how to bait him.

'Now, Danny, I'm sure Toby has a good reason to come today, be nice for once,' Mrs Sabo said.

'It's his fault, I'm like this.'

'Don't see how? Your father and uncle did this, Son. Not Toby.'

'Like I said Farrier. Rack off and don't come back. And you'd better stay outa my way when I get out, because I'm gunna get what I need and you can be damned sure there won't be any coppers around to protect you next time.' Slasher picked up the mug of water and hurled it in Toby's direction. 'Piss off I said...Now!'

Toby ducked the cup, 'you want my book; you can have it. It's got nothing important in it and nothing a dumb turd like you would ever be able to understand anyway.' He pulled the ledger from his backpack, throwing it at his rival. Slasher wheezed as the book hit his chest, yellowing pages puffing out a cloud of dust as it landed.

Slasher took a minute to get his breath. 'Go, I said.'

Toby turned his back, raised his middle finger and walked out. He'd never felt as alone as in those few minutes. Mrs Sabo hadn't said a thing; she'd just let Slasher rant. Pop was wrong, she was just another stinking Sabo.

CHAPTER TWENTY-FOUR

Toby didn't want to go home, there was no one there. He couldn't call in to see Sophia, she was away with her family, and his mates were doing other stuff. He pushed every button in the elevator, slumped in the corner and wept. Minutes passed like days and then, there it was again. The same scent he had smelled earlier. A hand reached out to touch him, Toby didn't resist and he tilted his head so he could see the stranger.

'Toby, is it you? My God, how you've grown.'

He'd know his estranged stepmother's voice anywhere.

'What are you doing here, what's wrong? Is Arthur alright?' Her questions peppered him. 'Have you been crying?'

'Tracy?' Toby stood, opened his arms and sunk against her. The elevator stopped and he looked up into her eyes. 'I smelt your perfume in the lift earlier, but thought it must have been someone else.' He backed away and picked up his bag. 'Pop's fine, I came to see a kid from school, and let's just say he didn't want to see me.'

Although her clothes were immaculate, he could tell she'd been crying too. 'Are you sick Trace, why are you here?'

'I was just coming down to phone you and Artie again,' she said. 'I've tried several times. Left messages, but he's not answering. It was when I saw you in the lift just now and, I don't know, I thought perhaps he was unwell too.' Tracy blurted the words, then her tears flowed.

The word *too,* rattled in and around a thousand thoughts, 'Pop's all good, why do you want him?' he heard the urgency in his words.

'Your dad was bringing a load of sheep home last night and had a huge accident. He's been in Emergency since midnight. They're saying it's serious, and a couple of hours ago, his doctors asked me to let his family know.'

All Toby could do was nod. He thought about the past and tried to remember the good times they shared; however, the only thing that raced in a loop through his mind was, what if he dies and we never get to know each other again?

Tracy was still whispering. 'Toby I'm so frightened for him. What'll I do without my best friend?'

'Where are the kids?'

'They're with the neighbours today, but I'll need to sort something out for tomorrow.'

'Can I see him?'

'Sure, but he's comatose, with tubes and wires everywhere. It's fairly confronting.'

'I saw Slash that way, I know what to expect.' Toby ran his hand down her arm.

'And, what about Arthur?'

'I'll find him. But first, I want to see my dad.'

CHAPTER TWENTY-FIVE

Darren Farrier appeared lifeless, his breathing controlled by a ventilator, his head swollen and bruised made him appear grotesque. Tubes and wires led to machines where coloured lines danced across monitors. Nurses and doctors fussed around him, no one noticed Toby enter the ward.

'Is he...' Toby said.

'I don't know,' Tracy answered. 'Right now, they're trying to stabilise him enough to release the pressure around his brain. We can't do much here, but you can help me find Arthur. He needs to know...' She stopped and put her hand over her mouth, turned and walked away from the ward.

Toby finished the sentence for her. 'In case he doesn't make it?'

Tracy just nodded.

'We'd better find Pop; he'll be at Charlie's.'

Toby ignored the closed sign and pushed on the door. 'Mr Ramsey, Pop, are you here?'

'Yeah, up here.' Charlie's voice echoed down the stairs.

'Pop, can you come down, there's someone to see you?'

'Bring him up here. Your legs are younger than mine.'

Toby waved for Tracy to lead the way, and at the top of the landing she stopped at the kitchen door.

Arthur could only see her shadow, but knew it was her. 'Tracy, what is it, what brings you here?'

'It's Darren... The police say he tried to miss a car that crossed onto his side of the freeway. Steering to miss them, his rig crashed off the road last night.' Tracy took a couple of deep breaths. 'Arthur, I'm sorry, but he's smashed up really bad. His doctors have told me to get the family together.' She turned away and said, 'In case he...'

Arthur stood and put a hand on her shoulder. She turned into him and he embraced her. 'Okay, we know he's a tough one.' One hand rubbed her back the other held her. 'And he'll be fighting, but if that's what they've said we'd better go.'

'Thanks, I know things are...'

Arthur put his hands on her shoulders and eased her back enough, so they could see into each other's eyes. 'Things that were said in the past can't be unsaid, but a Farrier family forgives,' he said. 'We're going to be alright, girl. You have to believe that. Darren was damn stubborn as a kid and I don't reckon he's changed. He'll be fighting this all the way. You'll see.'

'He looks bad though, Arthur.'

'I expect he does, Trace. I expect he does.'

'Can you sit with him for a while? I have to do some stuff with the business and there's people to call. Monday is fine, I've got the blokes organised, but Darren's truck, and trailers are still on the Hume, and then there's the kids.'

'Look, we'll go to the hospital and work it out from there. Don't worry, you let us know what needs doing and then Charlie and me will make calls. We'll do whatever, okay?' Arthur smiled. 'I can tell you're wearing that perfume Darren likes.'

'My J-Adore...I don't know why I picked it for today. Maybe I thought it would remind him of happier times. Maybe I wore it for me. Maybe I didn't want to remember the stench of a stock-crate full of sheep. I don't know.'

'Well, I like it,' Toby said. 'Come on let's get back to Dad.'

Arthur placed a hand on Toby's shoulder. 'I think you'd better stay here for now, that's if it's okay with Charlie?'

'We'll be fine, do whatever has to be done and we'll see you back at your place.' Charlie said.

Toby stared at the floor. He hated it when they left him out. Charlie suggested he go home and make up a couple of spare beds, saying that if Tracy and the kids needed to stay, then the house would be ready. He said would lock up and follow later.

Toby couldn't work out why, but as he walked along his street, he felt another tingle rush through him. The hair on his neck stood on end, and something inside his head told him to stay away from the house. He crossed to the opposite side of the road, pulled his collar up and walked past their home. He turned the corner and saw the same silver car that was parked in the street before, but now it was on the other side of the road. No one around here drove anything like that, it was empty and yet it made him feel uneasy. He tried to look into their house, but the trees lining the street hid it. Something moved near the front gate. Whoever owned the Audi, must be the same person who tried to steal his book. A red alarm light blinked on the Audi's dash and it gave him an idea. Toby removed a valve cap from the front tyre and removed the black rubber that exposed the valve tool. A couple of anti-clockwise turns and the tyre eased a gentle hiss. One down three to go, it was the work of seconds.

At the end of the block, Toby crossed the street and took the former night-cart lane that ran along the back of the houses. If he prised off a couple of loose palings from the back fence he could sneak in and surprise their visitor.

Weeds tangled around a metre length of rusty pipe at the bottom of the fence, and he was about to give up on the idea, when the first board gave way. He pulled at the second and opened a hole big enough to squeeze through. On his hands and knees, he studied the house. Splintered wood and a torn screen showed him someone had jemmied the back door. He wanted to race in, subdue the burglar and phone the police, but he calmed himself. Toby watched for a minute or two, nothing was moving. Maybe the burglar had gone.

Satisfied it was safe, Toby started to climb through the hole. He felt his arm almost snap as someone pulled him up, and thrust him face first against the fence. Pressure burned in the base of his spine as a knee drove into the middle of his back. He wanted to kick out, but the weight holding him onto the palings was too much.

'I want my book you little turd. Where is it?'

'What book?'

'O'Toole's diary, I know you have it.' There was the smell of whisky on the man's breath and his accent had traces of posh about it.

'Who are you?'

The knee leaned in harder and the fence creaked. Now the hand shoved his face into the railing again. 'It doesn't matter who I am, I just want that damned book.'

'Go to hell.' Toby didn't swear often, but he was past angry. His lips contorted from the pressure, he wanted to turn and spit on his attacker, but couldn't. A distorted, 'it's mine, Ryan,' was all he could manage. This guy had to be the professor that Mr Wyatt mentioned; and by using his name Toby hoped for affirmation. It had to be him, who else knew anything about this?

'You'll get it for me, even if I have to drag you to it on your backside.' The man spun him off the fence and tried to throw him against the palings again. This time Toby slipped his head down and ducked the rail. The palings gave way, and the attacker's grip loosened as he lost his balance. The man's head crashed into the top rail, the skin on his forehead ripped, tearing back along his hairline.

Toby rolled out into the lane, jumped to his feet and looked at his adversary sprawled half way through the fence. Toby was free, but Ryan, if that's who he was, was dazed. The man started to stir, Toby picked up the pipe and crashed it down onto the back of Ryan's head. Blood spurted from the wound, and for Toby, time seemed to slow. A mist of red drifted up at him. Toby felt the warm and sticky ooze stick to his face, his mouth was open and he could taste Ryan's blood. He squinted trying to focus, but now his glasses were spotted with crimson and it blurred his view. Ready to strike another blow he lifted the pipe again, then he heard something deep and slow. Someone was screaming, but everything had morphed into freeze frame. The weapon swung down one more time. The crack of iron on Ryan's skull sounded like lightning and he felt the jar run up into his hands. Skin and hair parted in a tangle of red muck, for a moment a white line appeared and was gone. It seemed like minutes, but Toby knew it was over in a flash.

Someone grabbed his arms, pinning them. 'Toby, no more.'

Toby turned to look at him. 'Mr Wyatt?'

The teacher shook his head. 'He's done, he's had enough.' He let go and Toby dropped the pipe. 'I guess you have now met Professor Ryan.' he dragged Ryan back through the rails, pulled out his phone and began calling triple zero.

Charlie panted and heaved his way toward the crumpled figure on the ground. 'What's going on? Who is he? Who are you?' He held his walking stick as if it were a sword against the teacher's jugular, demanding he explain.

'I'm okay, Charlie,' Toby said, 'I noticed this bloke's car in the street and I thought he was in the house. When I came through the fence, he jumped me. I don't know why, but after that I just wanted to keep hitting him.' Toby turned to Wyatt. 'Sorry Sir.'

'Sir?' Charlie asked, still pointing his stick at the teacher.

'Sure, this is Mr Wyatt, my English teacher.'

'Well who the hell is this then?' The walking stick knocked into Ryan's knee.

'Professor Phillip Ryan,' Wyatt answered, 'but why he's here is for him to explain.'

Charlie rested on his stick, 'you reckon he's out to it, or just playing possum?'

'I don't think he'll worry us at present. Toby you'd be best to stay still until the ambulance gets here.'

'But why are you here,' Toby asked, his mind still racing from the adrenaline, 'how did you know this bloke was in the house?

William Wyatt shifted from one foot to the other and back again, 'I called in to see Slash... I mean Danny Sabo and they showed me a book you left with them. I recognised your sketch as Professor Ryan and wondered why you'd have drawn and dated it today. When they said you left in a hurry, I wondered why.' His voice was racing through the words as if he had little time to spare. He slowed and running a hand through his hair, drew in a couple of deep breaths, 'I just wanted to check on you, that's all.'

Before he could say any more, an ambulance arrived in the lane. Paramedics swarmed around the professor, checking his condition before stabilising him enough to load him into the ambulance.

They turned their attention to Toby who was trying to recollect everything that had happened. He tried to stand, but faltered. 'Our back door has been forced and I need to see inside,' Toby said, as a paramedic applied a swab to his face and started removing splinters.

'I'll phone the police,' Wyatt said.

'No need.' Constable John Evans stepped through the hole in the fence and into the lane. Another police officer followed him through. 'This is Constable Jenny Azzopardi.' He knelt down to meet Toby's eyeline. 'You're attracting a lot of attention lately, mate. After we've checked the house, you can tell us what's been going on, okay?'

Dropping his eyes Toby said, 'yeah, thanks.'

Evans nodded toward the ambulance where Ryan was laying on a gurney, a paramedic was monitoring his condition. 'Find out how he's doing, then we'll work out what to do next.'

'Sounds like a plan.' Her voice was melodic and warm. She turned toward Toby. 'Now what causes a kid like you to beat up on a bloke in his fifties?' She narrowed her eyes and he felt the freeze of her stare. He looked away, and thought how first impressions can sometimes be wrong.

CHAPTER TWENTY-SIX

Charlie muttered as he hammered and bashed in an attempt to repair the fence. 'Twenty years ago, I'd have ripped that bastard to bits.' He smashed another nail into a board, it split and he cursed even more. 'I'd teach him to pick on a fifteen-year-old kid, and there'd be no need for coppers when I'd finished with him.' He struck the fence again and it shook under the mallet's force. 'I'd beat him to a pulp and feed him through a hammer mill. Spread him like fertiliser so no one would find him, just foxes and crows to pick up his pieces.' The fence juddered every time he swung the hammer to emphasise his words.

Toby watched him and wished it had been Charlie who'd dealt with Ryan.

Charlie looked up as though he'd sensed Toby watching him. 'You fixed up okay?

'I'm fine, but like you said, I've Have to get the house ready in case Tracy and the kids come to stay.'

Charlie looked into Toby's eyes. 'You'd like that?'

'Yeah, I reckon so.' Toby rubbed his arm and shifted his weight from one foot to the other. He swayed and leaned on the fence. For a moment, he felt woozy and pushing the palms of his hands onto the fence, he slid onto the ground. He felt cold and rubbed both hands up and down his arms. Soon shivering started and to control it, he pulled his legs up to his chest and wrapped his arms around them.

'Over here!' Charlie yelled. 'It's Toby. Come right now. Leave that bastard,' he shouted. 'I need some help over here, something's wrong with our boy.'

A paramedic rushed to Toby's side and felt his head.

'Get a blanket around him.' One of the green uniforms yelled.

Toby shivered and shook, he couldn't comprehend what was happening to him, but he felt safe. A sharp prick in his arm. Soothing words. Cool fluid into his arm. He closed his eyes. All he wanted was to go to sleep, but voices were pleading with him to stay awake. Saying his name over and again.

Toby heard Sophia talking to Charlie. He struggled to open his eyes. 'Soph, what are you doing here?' He reached for her hand.

'All the lights and cars down here... I thought you'd done something stupid and I was worried.' She leaned in and kissed his cheek. 'You frightened me, you dork.'

Her lips were warm and soft. Toby sensed a funny quiver in his body, and he liked it. He wiped a tear from her cheek.

He sat up and saw the police were still there. 'The bloke who grabbed me, did he get into the house?' Toby's stare fixed on the policeman. 'And where is he now? Did he get away? It's the same bloke who slapped me at the library. Isn't it?'

'You're safe now, kid. We have him all tucked up in the ambulance. He's not going anywhere.'

'Did he take anything?' Toby focused on Constable John Evans. 'Does Pop know?'

'Arthur's on his way home now,' Charlie said. 'I phoned him a minute ago, Tracy and the kids are coming tonight. Even if the house is a mess, we'll put it right before they get here, won't we Soph?'

'Yes, but is Toby going to hospital?' She sniffed and squeezed Toby's hand.

'Not now, I wouldn't recommend doing too much, but once he gets something inside him, he'll be fine. That okay with you, young man?'

Toby shielded his eyes, he looked at the paramedic kneeling alongside him. 'Will I need to keep this in?' He raised his arm attached to the saline drip.

'We'll take it out when the bag's empty. Then you can stay home, but it's rest for the remainder of the day. Do we have a deal?'

'Sure, but do I hafta just sit around?'

'That's the deal.'

The drip now empty, the ambulance officers removed the line and helped Toby into the lounge room. Toby grinned as they explained to Sophia, how she should care for him over the next few hours.

CHAPTER TWENTY-SEVEN

Toby wanted to help, and having to rest frustrated him. Today's events of ran around in his mind. The bloke who ransacked his study must be the same one who attacked him in the street. His head hurt, and all he wanted to do was visit his dad in hospital. Arthur returned just as Charlie and Sophia had everything ready for Tracy and the family to stay.

'I did what I could with your study Tobe, but you'll need to go through your stuff and sort it out later.' Sophia shuffled along the couch until she moulded into Toby's side. Her hand cupped his chin as she turned his face to hers and looked at the bruises. 'Poor baby,' she said. 'Look what the nasty man did to your face.' She stretched toward him and with wet lips touched the bruise. 'I'll kiss it better for you.'

Toby held the back of her neck and let his lips explore hers.

'You kids okay in there?' They heard Arthur coming from the kitchen. 'We'll order takeaway when Trace gets here.'

Sophia and Toby recoiled from their clinch.

'Works for me.' The smirk on Toby's face would have given them away had Arthur reached the room. 'I vote for pizza,' he said.

'What about Chinese? Charlie's paying.' They could hear Arthur pop the top of his home brew. 'I'll order when they get here.'

'You nearly got me into trouble then Toby, what were you thinking?' Sophia hissed, stood and straightened her clothes.

'I don't know? Didn't you want me too?'

'Yeah but...'

'But what?'

'I don't know, we're friends and all, but here's you sitting there all forlorn and beaten up. I guess I realised you mean more to me than just being friends...' Her face flushed, but she kept looking at him as though she was waiting for him to say something.

'Me too, but we'll need to stay cool until things settle down a bit.' He squeezed her hand. 'Let's go to my room, the old fellas can't hear as much from there.' He felt a giggle in his voice and tried to suppress it, but knew his grin wouldn't leave his face.

Toby stopped at his study. Sophia had stacked everything into piles on the floor. Splinted wood near the lock of the desk showed the intruder forced it, the normally taught rolls were skewed and limp.

'I'll get the bastard for this. I don't know why, but I feel worse about him smashing my desk than my face.' Toby began to shake, he recognised his anger, something he hadn't felt for years was coming back, and he didn't like it.

'You'd better go Soph, thanks for the help today.' His hand on the small of her back turned her toward the door.

'What is wrong with you, Farrier? A minute ago, we're making out and everything, and now you're behaving like a prat. I thought you liked me?'

'It's me I don't like at the moment. You wouldn't understand. Just go home and stay there. I'm not someone you want to be with right now.' He slapped the door frame, he felt pain in his hand and liked it.

Sophia dropped her head.

'I can't have you hanging around feeling sorry for me. I don't need your pity, Soph. I don't need anyone. Just go home.' He couldn't stop the words coming and wanted to swallow his tongue to stop them. Sophia hadn't caused this. He knew it wasn't his fault, and yet he couldn't stop the meanness overtaking him.

'You're a creep, Toby Farrier.' Tears gave way to anger. 'You don't deserve the few friends you do have, and you certainly don't deserve me.' She stormed through the house slamming the porch door on her way out.

Arthur stormed down the passage and stopped in the door to Toby's room. 'What was all that about? What happened to make Soph rush out like that? We know you were necking on the couch in there. Did you touch her where you shouldn't?'

The accusations stung him, but Toby said nothing.

Arthur rubbed his arm. 'I know I haven't said much to you about the birds and bees, but for pity's sake boy, Sophia is one respectable little lady.' Arthur frowned. 'I thought you were better than that, Tobe.'

'It's nothing like that, Pop. I like her more than I knew. It's just that I lost it. I thought about the bloke who belted me and it fired me up. I'm angry inside and when I was hitting him, all I wanted to do was beat him into a mess and leave him for dead. I felt those old demons raging around inside me again, urging me to do something I'd regret.' As his words poured out, a shiver ran through him and looking down, he saw he was twisting his knuckle into his left palm. 'Pop, I'm scared. Look.' Holding his hand out. 'I know this is a coping mechanism, but I haven't done it since you rescued me from Kyneton.' Just getting his words out helped and he could feel relief washing his tension away. Take a few slow deep breaths and find your inner core he told himself. After a minute or two, he had control.

'Son, things were tough on you as a kid. There'll be times when people push you to that point again, but you're a good lad and you know right from wrong. I reckon I'd want to do the same things to him too. It's not demons from your past, but anger from what happened today. You should be angry, but search for justice, not revenge, and never confuse the two.' He sat on the bed alongside him. Toby leant against him. Arthur reached an arm around his grandson's shoulders and squeezed. 'Okay Son?'

'Okay, but it frightened me, Pop.'

Yeah, well that's as it may be, but what about Sophia, she needs an explanation too.'

'Soph?'

'Yes Sophia, now get moving, run after her and tell her what you've just told me. Tell her why you came to live with me. Leave nothing out. She'll understand why you are who you are, and why you're worth it.' Arthur stood up, put his hand on Toby's shoulder and looked into his eyes. 'She needs to know why you acted like that. Later when everyone's settled in, Tracy can take you and Sophia into the hospital, okay?'

'Yep, you make a lot of sense for an old bloke, Pop.' The cloud that had dogged his mind for years seemed to lift and he felt his grin come back. 'Think we might get our family together again, Pop?'

'I hope so, Son, I hope so. Off with you now and bring that young lady back, she makes old fellas like me and Charlie feel young again.'

Toby heard the backdoor slam behind him as he ran up the street.

CHAPTER TWENTY-EIGHT

Toby could see Sophia ahead and his feet felt lighter. They sometimes walked through the park rather than take the short way up the street. Although he could see she had her arms crossed and was stomping more than walking, he knew if he could apologise everything was going to be okay. He called to her, but she didn't seem to hear. As he sped up to get closer a person dashed out of from the bushes ahead and started chasing her. He felt sick. Was it the Ryan guy again? It couldn't be. He was in the ambulance last time they saw him and besides, the cops had said they had him in custody. No time to think. Sophia was in trouble. He pushed his legs harder and that familiar ball of anger surged. She started running faster, but the figure chasing her was gaining. He had to catch whoever it was before they harmed his Sophia.

Toby's speed was greater and when he drew level he kicked as the figure's leg followed through, the trip sending them sprawling along the path. He jumped into the middle of the figure's back and began punching at the individual writhing below him. All of the anger he'd felt earlier was boiling out of him now and even though his fists were hurting, relief came with every pound as vengeance danced through them.

Sophia's voice cut through. 'Toby, what are you doing?' She grabbed his arm and dragged him off.

The shape was a man, with Toby's weight off he groaned, rolled over and stood up. They backed away. They couldn't see the face properly, but from under his hood the streetlight glistened on a line of blood running from the cut above his right eye. The only other thing Toby could see was his cheek had blood dotting scrape lines where he assumed it had scraped the footpath when they fell.

He snarled at them. 'You little bastards are going to pay for this.'

Toby felt for something to use as a weapon, his hand felt a stake that had once supported a shrub, and he swung it at their attacker. Stepping back from the swing the thug's hands followed the stake, snatching it. A sharp pull and Toby over balanced and fell forward.

Grabbing Toby by the arm he ripped it up behind his back. 'A bit of a smartarse, aren't you kid? Well you won't know what hit you this time.' He spun Toby around and held him by the collar. 'Righto kid, say goodbye to your girl, because you'll never see her again.' He dropped the stake and drew his fist back.

Toby closed his eyes expecting pain. Instead he felt the grip on his collar loosen and as he fell back, he heard Sophia scream. Opening his eyes he watched the evil bastard swing, smashing the stake into her ribs. The timber cracked as it jarred her frame, knocking her backwards and landing on top of him.

As he caught his breath, he saw the figure half running, half limping into the shadows. Toby could feel Sophia gasping for breath. he struggled, untangling his arms and legs, trying to get out from under her. He wiped his mouth with the back of his hand, and tilted her head back. Sophia thrashed out, her legs kicking and her arms flailing trying to push him away, but he knew people in Soph's state needed help. He knelt down, sealed his mouth on hers, and blew with all his might.

Sophia wriggled free and rolled away from him. 'Get off me, Farrier, you dope. What the hell were you doing? Cripes I was only winded; sometimes you amaze me Toby.' She felt the giggle coming and as she shook, her chest and arms hurt. 'You don't find many people drowning on dry land.'

'Yeah, well I could see you had the wind knocked out of you, and I thought the kiss of life would help to get you going again.' He stood up, stretched and reached out to help her to her feet. 'I saw him coming after you and just went wild. I didn't want him to hurt you.'

'Really?' she said making sure there was a hint of sarcasm in her tone, 'I didn't think you wanted to see me for a while?'

He looked at his watch. 'It's been well over three minutes.' Toby let a grin flash across his face, it felt good. 'Should be long enough, I reckon.'

Their assailant had gone, but it was dark, they were alone and Sophia was injured. Toby put his arm around her and said. 'We'd better get you some help.'

Sophia nodded.

'Here let's have a look at you.' Toby said turning her hands toward the light.

Sophia moved into a sliver of streetlight that searched its way through the trees. 'My bag, it's gone.'

He heard trembling in her voice.

'Did he snatch it?' Toby's voice raised a couple of octaves and he tried to calm himself. He didn't need Sophia to panic, she was in plenty of bother as it was. 'I'll have a look around.' He dropped to his knees and reached out; small stones now dug in where his weight centred on them. He sifted the leaf litter and felt the leather strap of the bag, he tugged but the bush held it. 'I've got it, just have to untangle it first.' He tried to weave the strap out of the leaves but that just made it worse. 'Nearly there, I just have to move in a bit.' He shifted position and then he felt it. Once the dried surface broke the foul smell raced into his nostrils. The ooze squelched through his fingers. 'Aaghhh, dog poop.' Could his day get any worse?

'Don't touch my bag then, I'll get it.' Sophia crouched and reached through the bushes. 'You're more than just a mate, Toby. You do know that, don't you?' She dragged her bag from the bush and stood up. 'But right now, you really stink.' Sophia tried to laugh, but holding an arm across her chest winced and groaned instead. 'Geeze my hands hurt, and... the side of my chest.'

Toby dragged his hands through the leaves of the shrub to remove the dog dirt. 'People who don't pick up their dog's business should be locked up,' he said.

'Here, I've got tissues. Use them.' Sophia reached in, but she cried out. 'Damn it Farrier, why did you have to get poop all over you? These damn splinters.' She strained and with her thumbs, prised the bag open. 'Here, reach in there, they're in a soft pack.' Toby moved closer. 'And not with the dirty hand either.'

Toby rummaged inside her bag, there were all kinds of stuff in there that he didn't even want to think about. He found a soft pack and held it up.

'No, put it back. The tissues are in the side pocket,' She pushed him aside. 'Get out of there, I'll do it myself. Here.' She pulled a few tissues out and thrust it into his clean hand. 'Clean yourself up.'

Toby wiped his hand and tossed the tissue on the ground.

'You can't leave that there. Put it in the bin.'

The acid in Sophia's words burned deep into his ears and as he reached for the spent paper, his fingers touched a small cardboard box. He picked it up and shook it. 'This yours?' He held the box up.

'No, come on I want to go home.'

Toby thought about throwing the box away when he dumped the tissues, but wondering what it was, slipped it into his pocket. Sophia was doubled over and clutching her chest. They stopped under the streetlight to get a better look at the splinters in her hands. If they could get them out, it might stop some of her pain. Toby turned her palms toward the light, a piece of jagged timber about thirty millimetres long, wedged under the skin, it went from the heel of her right thumb all the way to the first joint. Several smaller splinters peppered her palm. Her left hand was similar, but there were no big chunks.

'We need tweezers, or a needle, or something.' Toby let her hands go and eased Sophia more into the light. 'You're bleeding.'

'Where?'

He pointed at her shirt.

She looked down where Toby's finger pointed. 'How bad is it? Is anything sticking into me.' She tried to lift the shirt, but cried out. 'I can't close my hands. You'll have to do it.'

Toby listening to her breathing becoming shallow and laboured, said. 'I reckon I should get you home, it's not far.'

'Just do it Tobe.' Her words sounded to strangle in her throat. 'Just look at the wound though, not my boobs.' She said, putting an arm across her chest.

Toby lifted one side of her shirt. There was blood. Lots of blood. He dropped it. 'Let's get you home... Now.'

CHAPTER TWENTY-NINE

The porchlight was on when Toby and Sophia reached the Nguyen home. Toby shrugged to hitch Sophia's arm higher around his shoulders as he reached for the doorbell. Before his finger touched the button, the door swung open and seeing the look on Mrs Nguyen's face made his heart sink. Behind her he could see anger in her dad's eyes, if anyone could feel any lower or more worthless, he doubted it. However, Sophia needed help.

'What you do my girl?' Ahn's broken English coming like machinegun fire.

'Dad.' Sophia pushed the word out as she slipped her arm away and drooped into her mother's arms. 'Toby saved me.'

'You better wait outside, Toby Farrier.' Ahn was still angry.

'Don't listen to him Toby, come in and say to us what happened,' Sophia's mother said.

Sophia and her mother went through to the kitchen while Toby followed with Ahn behind him. Mr Nguyen grabbed the phone, 'I call police?'

'No-no-no, Ahn. Ambulance first.' Mrs Nguyen was pointing her finger at him, she looked back over her shoulder to Toby saying, 'and you, you wait for them while I look at Sophia.'

Toby was in no hurry to argue, but he was concerned about the attack, 'I'll wait on the porch.' He left them to it and waited outside for the ambulance and police.' He thought he understood why she had walked through the park. It had always been safe and he and his friends often crossed it after dark. He felt another shiver and wondered if it was still shock from earlier. His thoughts returned to Sophia, why was she singled out for attack, was it opportune or something more sinister?'

'Police be here soon, you come inside now, we wait together.' Ahn's anger had subsided, he ushered Toby into the front living room and waved for him to sit on the couch. Ahn took the armchair alongside the fireplace, he had a quizzical look on his face.

Toby thought the accent in his broken English was disappearing.

'Why did our Sophia come across the park?'

'I don't know, I was angry, I said some stuff and told her to leave.'

'But you followed her?'

'I was sorry about what I said.'

'How you know she go that way.'

'Pop said he saw her heading into the park...'

Before he could say more, there was a knocking on the door and when Ahn opened it, he felt as if the alternating strobes of blue and red light were stabbing him as they filled the passageway. Toby had to blink a few times to stabilise his senses. When he opened his eyes again, he saw Mr Nguyen ushering the Ambulance officers toward the kitchen.

In his heart he wanted to follow, but knew Sophia would not want him there. Leaning back on the couch he closed his eyes, trying to remember everything that had happened up until this minute. He knew the police would be asking questions the moment they arrived, and staying away from Sophia would allow him to recall the vents as they happened.

'Toby,' He knew the voice, opening his eyes Constable Evans towered over him. 'you okay mate?'

'A few more bruises that's all, but Soph's not good.'

'I'll take a look,' Constable Azzopardi was with him. 'And look, sorry about before, I had the wrong end of the stick.'

Over the next hour Toby recounted everything that had happened since the police left his home that afternoon. However, two questions burned hard in his mind, was it the Ryan bloke who attacked her and if so, why wasn't he locked up?

'We can't say who it was Toby,' John Evans rubbed a hand through his hair, 'but while we were talking to you, Ryan let himself out of the ambulance. We've lost him for now.'

'Pop's in danger then.' Toby pushed his hands into the couch. 'Whatever that creep wanted he hasn't got it yet.'

'Easy Tiger,' John said as Toby stood up, 'We'll take you home as soon as we're finished here.'

'I can't wait,' he dodged past the policeman and toward the door, 'Pop needs to know where I've been.'

'Hang on, I'm coming with you.'

Toby went straight inside, the policeman followed. Relieved that Pop was okay, he started to feel exhaustion consuming him. Arthur looked to loom in the hallway as though he was waiting for an explanation. Toby thinking the policeman could do all the explaining, just wanted to go to his room and rest.

'Nice to see you too Son...' Arthur called after him.

Toby left the door open, hoping to listen to everything Evans would say.

'G'day again,' The constable said, 'we are starting to make this place our second home.'

'Sure, John, go through to the kitchen.' Arthur waved and pointed to the door. 'We have my daughter in law and her children with us at the moment. The kids are hungry and I was just about to order takeaway, do you mind if I do that first.'

'Yeah, go for it. Jen and I want to have another look at Toby's room, to see if we can find a reason for the break in today.'

'Is Sophia okay, what's happened? No wait, I'll get Charlie onto organising dinner. Then you can tell me everything.'

Toby turned over on his bed and pushed his face deep into the pillow. He didn't need to hear anything more. The whole day had been too much. At least he knew Sophia was going to be okay now. However, Tracy being here with the kids allowed a few doubts to begin chipping away at his confidence, and he began rolling them over in his mind. Tracy will probably think all of this is his fault. He shut his eyes and breathed out slowly until he heard Arthur clear his throat.

'You okay?'

Toby nodded and sat up. 'Why would he want to hurt Soph, Pop. I know we are supposed to stay out of the park, but we cross it all the time and nothing's ever happened before.'

Arthur shook his head. 'Don't know mate. Why don't you come out to the kitchen with the others? Tracy and the kids are here.'

Toby followed Arthur down the hall to the kitchen. Arthur sat at the table.

Tracy leant on Arthur's chair. 'Grand day for a family reunion, eh?' She smiled a grimace at the constable. 'Is Toby in trouble again?'

Toby scowled. 'That's it isn't it, you always thought I was no good and now you want to put yourself between me and Pop. I should've known when I saw you at the hospital, that all you wanted was to look after your own kids.' He felt his eyes burning with the same contempt he felt the day they turned him out. He was bigger stronger and more aware now. He lunged at her.

Evans held him back and grabbed his hands and forced them to his sides. 'Hey man, that's not what she meant, and you know it.' John relaxed his grip. 'Let it all out, Toby.' His hands rubbed Toby's back in a soft and circular motion.

Toby clenched his teeth.

'You're an okay kid, we have to get to the bottom of what's going on here, that's all.'

Constable Azzopardi cleared her throat and waited until everyone was looking at her. 'About half an hour ago, Sophia was attacked in the park. If Toby hadn't come to help her... I'm not sure what would have happened.' She picked up a glass from the rack above the sink and raised it. 'May I?'

'Yeah, sure.' Arthur said.

'I didn't mean it to come out the way it did, Arthur, I truly didn't.' Tracy said.

Arthur nodded.

Jenny up turned the glass and set it on the sink. 'Anyway, with all that's happened today, John and I wanted to have another look in Toby's room, if that's okay with you, Toby?'

Toby nodded.

'We'd like to look at his study too, try to find reasons for both attacks. You know, see if they're linked. Toby didn't get a good look at their attacker and Sophia only said he was an evil looking bloke in a hoodie.' She could have been describing anyone.

Toby shoved his hands deep into his pockets, turned his toes in and dropped his eyes. He should have taken more notice of the deadbeat, then the police could find him. He felt the box in his pocket. He'd forgotten all about it and taking it out, handed the box to Evans.

'I found this where Soph was attacked, it could have fallen out of his pocket.' He shrugged as John studied it. 'Sorry, it's covered in my fingerprints and probably a fair bit of dog doo.'

Evans turned it over. 'No dog doo, thank goodness, but this is interesting.' He passed the box to his partner who read the name on the label.

She raised one eyebrow. 'Indeed. Very interesting. Should I bag it, you reckon?'

'Not now, I don't think we'll need to check it for prints. There'll be DNA on the mouth piece if it gets that far.' Evans smiled and put his hand on Toby's shoulder. Good work.' He winked at Tracy. 'Told you he was doing okay.'

'You know Tracy?' Toby felt his mouth drop open.

'Yep.'

'How?'

'It's a long story, but a good one. Let's get this bloke and then we'll all have a sit down when your dad's awake.' John winked at him, 'you'll like the story mate, I promise.'

Jenny looked around. 'Toby, I know I've asked you a hundred different ways, but the attack on you today, can you give me any clue as to why this person ransacked your study? What do you think he was looking for?'

'I dunno. Like I said, I thought someone was in the house so I came through the back. He must have seen me, or there might have been two of them, I just don't know.'

Tracy held her hand up and said. 'That's enough for today, my son has been through a fair bit and I think it's time you left him alone. Give him some time to have dinner and get to know his sisters and me.'

Toby wondered if he heard properly, did Tracy just say, *my son?*

CHAPTER THIRTY

Toby stirred in his chair and rubbed his eyes. Tracy's arm lay along Darren's hospital bed, with her head half on, half off the pillow. Her face was drawn, and the pillow had stain spots where her tears pooled. He thought about how today's events had taken their toll and pushing his own feelings to the back of his mind, tried to recall the good times they had shared. Before he had fallen asleep, he remembered pulling his chair close to hers, their shoulders almost touching. He remembered too, that how as a kid he'd liked the way her fingers felt as she stroked his hair to soothe him and how it made him sleepy.

A nurse came to check Darren's observation chart, Toby looked across at his stepmother, tear stains marked her face. He stood up and moving alongside her, put an arm around her shoulder. She leant her head against his chest and without understanding why, he found himself stroking her hair.

'It's okay Trace,' he said. 'he's going to be okay. Cry if you need to, I'll be here for as long as it takes.

'I know mate.' She rubbed her hand along Darren's arm. 'I love him so much.' Her sobs were beginning to shake them both, and Toby had to shift his feet to maintain his balance. 'You and Arthur have so much going on right now, and we come along and drop all this onto you.'

'We're family, aren't we? Like Pop said, it's what families do.'

'But it's been so long. We hardly know you after…' She looked away. 'you came to live with Arthur. Darren, he—'

'Let's just wait and see how he finds me when he comes out of this. We don't have to say this now. I'm not ready yet.'

'Okay, let's just wait 'til he's better.' She twisted away and looked at her husband.

Toby thought how childlike she looked as she dragged her sleeve across her nose and sniffed. He pulled a couple of tissues from the dispenser on the wall and handed them to her.

'Ta.' She blew her nose and tucked the tissue into her sleeve. 'Now what's going on with this bloke who beat you? You want to talk about it?'

'Not really, there's some stuff I have to work out and I just need to go through it in my head first, okay?'

'Didn't mean to pry, just wanted to help that's all.'

'It's fine Trace. Pop got me this desk and I found an old book in it. Ever since then, someone's tried to take it from me. Must be because of the dead private investigator and what he found. The journal was inside, so it's mine, but this Professor Ryan bloke reckons it's his somehow. Mr Ramsay had it in storage for years, anyway we checked and it's all legit. So, even though it's mine, this bloody professor wants it.'

'Is he the same one who hurt Sophia?'

'I dunno. We didn't see him properly. It scares me though.'

'Hey,' Tracy said. 'I almost forgot. Why were you in here earlier?'

She was easy to talk to and he told her about Slasher's gang. Toby explained how he felt envious of the relationship Slash had with his mother and about his friends from school. They talked until the sun came up.

'Come on mate, I'd better get you home. Your dad isn't going to come out of this for a few days, and I know I need to get my head down for a while. We'll get some sleep, and you can come back later. Maybe you could tell him a few of your stories. I understand that reading or talking to people in his condition helps. You okay with that?'

'Can I give him something first?'

'Yeah sure, what've you got?'

Toby took the pen from his pocket and handed it to Tracy. She held it and rolled it around in her hand. The weight surprised her. She studied the gold filigree and the inscription. *From Z to S, Valentine's Day, 1929.'* Her fingers stroked the surface.

'I think he'd like it.' Tracy slipped it into the palm of Darren's hand and wrapped his fingers around it. 'Where'd you get it?'

'Came out of a secret panel in the desk. I love it, but it doesn't work. I wanted to give him something nice. Something of mine, for when he wakes up.'

Tracy put an arm around Toby's shoulder and walked him to the car. It didn't feel the same as he thought it would for Slasher, but the warmth, the smell and the touch of her made him tingle.

At home a million things sloshed back and forward in his mind, but most constant was Sophia. How soft and warm were her lips? More than once he ran his tongue over his own, searching for a taste of her, she was special. He cuddled his pillow and surrendered to dream.

CHAPTER THIRTY-ONE

At home and with the doors locked, Toby felt frustrated. He could take care of himself. All he wanted to do was see Sophia and find out how she was, but Pop had told him to stay home. Tracy had things to do in Kyneton and after breakfast she and the girls would head off. They would be back in a couple of hours, and then Toby was to take care of his sisters while she went to the hospital.

He felt hollow, he was hungry, but didn't want food. He didn't know what to do, or think about anything, and it wasn't boredom. He looked at the few notes he had made from the journal, but even Shamus O'Toole couldn't distract him enough to lighten his mood. Pop had some hard and fast rules about watching the television, unless football was on, so TV was out.

He went out to the fence where Charlie had nailed the palings back. Who was this Ryan bloke and why was he so intent on getting the journal? What was so important that he'd attack him for it? Toby had too many questions. The day dragged, he would see his dad later, but all he could do now, was wait.

It was after six o'clock when Tracy and the girls arrived back at the house, Pop trailed in behind them.

'We dropped into the hospital so the girls could see their dad, and the time got away from us.' Tracy said.

'You've been chasing through all that stuff about Shamus I suspect?' Pop said. 'How about we get Toby to rustle up some grub, girls?' Pop crouched down and held his arms out. They squealed as he hugged them.

'What do you reckon we should order, canned spaghetti or baked beans?'

Toby saw Tracy screw her nose up. 'We have eggs I could do poached eggs on toast,' he said.

'Yep, that's better girls isn't it?' their mother said.

'I'll have a can of beans with mine, thanks Tobe,' Arthur said. 'Oh, and make us a pot of tea too, Son. There's a good lad.'

Toby noticed the change in his grandfather. He was besotted with the little girls and loved having his family around him. Toby wondered if Pop's hopes might fail.

How could he feel so much alone in a house full of people? Toby lay in bed and tossed. He tried to slow his thoughts. The back door had never been locked in all the time he had lived there, they had always felt safe, but tonight was different. There was more than just Pop and him. Everything had changed and so Tracy had taken the spare key to let herself in. Pop was asleep and the girls were in the big bed in the spare room.

What was happening, and why now? It was all too hard to work out. All he wanted to do was talk to someone about his problems. He looked at the clock; it was too late to call Sophia. It made him smile to think about her. However, he needed to hear her voice to tell him she was okay.

CHAPTER THIRTY-TWO

Tracy and her girls were up and dressed when Toby dragged himself to the kitchen. Scruffing one hand through his hair and hitching up the back of his boxers with the other. He snuggled under the arm she put out for a hug, and wrapped both his arms around her bathrobe. She smelled nice.

'Hello,' he said. The words flowed from his mouth all thick and treacle like, but he didn't care. He had missed a mother's hugs and these would do. He looked at his halfsisters and asked them what they were doing today.

Before they could answer, Tracy said. 'Tobe, can you watch them this morning, I have some stuff with the business and a heap of e-mails to send to everyone. Darren usually replies to stuff like this, but I can't do it like he does.'

Toby nodded. 'I could give you a hand if you like. Send out a merged message to everyone.'

'No thanks mate, it's something I have to do myself anyway.'

Toby felt her rejection, but he'd offered. It was what Pop would expect him to do. He headed for the shower. With all these people in the house and his dad in hospital, everything was a distraction. He felt sore from the beating, and while he liked the way the water's warmth soothed his aches, it stung the open grazes on his skin. Bruises were turning purple and yellow edges started to show. Toby traced his finger around the outline of one on his pectoral muscle. Why not just give the bloke the book and save all the hurt? He'd never backed down from a fight before, but this was dragging friends and family in. It wasn't fair, the desk and everything in it, was his, Charlie had proved that. He lathered his hair and drew shapes on the steamed-up shower screen. He dawdled.

He jumped at Pop's voice yelling through the door. 'Come on mate. Other people need the bathroom.'

Toby snapped the shower closed and towelled himself dry, he didn't need to shave yet, but every day he checked the mirror, almost hoping to find a reason for a razor. He rubbed product into his hair and used his fingers to keep the blonde tips regular against his naturally black locks. He licked his index finger and ran it across his eyebrows. The mirror had almost cleared and he leaned toward it. One more check before he could catch up with Sophia to find out how she was coping.

He felt its throb the moment he saw it and touched it with the end of his little finger. The pain was sharp and made his eye hurt. He looked at it again, craning his neck, looking sideways and leaning as close to the mirror as he could. It was there all right, emerging from deep in the little crevice where his nostril met the inside of his cheek.

His first pimple. Toby stared at it for a minute and examined every detail. It felt as if it was getting bigger the more he watched it. He pulled back, his friends had zits and others made fun of them. Now he had one and he knew it would to happen to him too. Why today of all days? He wanted to look his best in case his dad woke up, but even more, he wanted to look good for Sophia. What could he do? He felt blank and wanted to hide in his room until it was gone.

'I'm done.' He called as he headed into his room and shut the door. What could he do? He pulled out his favourite pair of boxers and stepped into them, dropped the towel from his waist and slung it over the foot of his bed. Arthur opened the door and smiled at him. 'You're looking a bit spiffy for a bloke who took a hiding yesterday.'

'I thought I'd duck out, before Tracy leaves and see how Soph is getting on, you know after last night and all.' Toby wanted to avoid asking, but knew it was right. 'You don't mind, do you?'

'Best you stay home, at least for today mate. With all that's going on with your dad, I think you need to be here. Tracy's got a lot to do and you'll sit with the girls for her.'

'But Pop. I just want to see Soph, you know find out how she is and if the cops said anymore about the creep who attacked her.'

'Just help Trace today, thanks mate. Don't you want us to be all together again?'

'Yeah, I do, but being broken into and all, I must be close to whatever it is that Shamus was working on.'

'Damn it Toby, you've got to forget Shamus O'Toole. Whatever it is, it happened eighty years ago, everyone's dead. Look son, I know you think it's a big deal and I've been happy for you to have some fun with it, but it's time to move on. You're only a kid for Christ sakes and you've already been hurt. Better to let it go now, Toby. You understand me.'

'That's not fair, Pop.'

'Life's not fair Son, you of all people should know that.'

'Can I at least phone her then?'

'Yep, but help Tracy settle the girls first.'

Arthur sounded like a sergeant major from a movie. He hadn't spoken to Toby like this since their early days.

'I want to catch up with Charlie and go to the hospital. Trace has a lot of stuff she needs to do with the business, so you'll have to stay here and look after your sisters. Any plans you had for today will have to wait. You got that?'

'But Pop?'

'But nothing, mate. This is important. Just do as I say. No argument.'

Arthur's tone swamped Toby. He wanted to answer back, but knew it was no good. They shared the same stubborn trait and he felt the pressure of the conversation squeezing him. He tasted bile and tried to force back the anger rising inside him. All he could do was turn and flop face down on his bed. Could today get any worse?

'We'll give the girls your study while they're here too, okay? I'll get a couple of new beds or maybe a set of bunks for them. You know something pretty, the type of things little girls' like. It's not fair for Tracy to have to share her bed, she needs her space too.'

Toby could hear his grandfather's excitement and wished he could share it. However, his world was shrinking and taking his identity with it. A few days ago, it was just the two of them, now interlopers were pushing him out.

'You're okay with that, aren't you Tobe?'

Toby said nothing. He wanted to lash out and say something horrid, or break something, but held it in.

'Toby?'

'Pop.' He didn't look up. 'I'm fine with it.'

'Time you learnt to share, Son. It's what we do Toby, share.'

'The kids are in the lounge, they'll be alright for a while, but you'd better do the dishes as soon as you're dressed. When Tracy's out of the bathroom, best put on a load of washing too.' Arthur turned and then looked back at him. 'And you might ask if she needs some washing done, you could put it in with ours.'

Toby noticed a skip in the old fella's step, and as he walked away Toby said under his breath, 'Son to slave in less than a day.' He wished he could drag the words back before they hurt his grandfather, especially when he saw Arthur's eyes glare at him.

'Are you back-chatting me, boy?'

'Nah. I just thought of a title for a story I'm writing.'

CHAPTER THIRTY-THREE

Toby stacked the dishes and waited for Tracy to finish in the bathroom before running hot water into the sink. The door opened and steam wafted into the hallway. He heard Tracy say something to the girls in the lounge. Until now Pop had employed a policy of no television before five o'clock, and it grated that he made an exception for his sisters. Toby waited until the sink was full, and turned off the taps. He walked to Tracy's room and knocked on the open door-frame.

'Come in.'

'It's me Trace, are you dressed?'

'Near enough, you can come in.'

Toby saw a flash of skin coloured lace and he looked down at the floor as he felt his face flush with embarrassment. 'Pop said to ask if you wanted any washing done. I'm doing ours later, so I can put yours in at the same time if you like.

She gave him a wink and checked the image in the mirror. 'Do you separate the coloureds from the whites?'

Toby wanted to make some smart remark about discrimination, but resisted. 'Yep, Pop makes me segregate.'

Tracy looked herself up and down. 'Do I look okay?'

'Umm yeah, good.' He grinned at her. 'You look nice.'

'And here I was, hoping for knock out too.' Tracy reached over and gave his hair a scruff. 'I'll leave our stuff in the laundry for you.' She slipped into a pair of patent leather high heels. 'But, what do you really think? I have to talk with our insurers this morning and it always pays to dress the part.' She turned to one side and looked herself up and down again. 'I feel more powerful when I suit up,'

Toby knew the shoes were expensive; Sophia had pointed to a similar pair in the window of a high-end Sydney Road shop last week. She went on about them all the way home, and looking at his stepmother now, Toby was getting a better understanding of the pull that clothes and accessories had on women.

Tracy dabbed a little perfume from the bottle on the dressing table. 'Right, now I'm ready for war,' she said.

Toby stood at the sink rinsing off the suds and standing the dishes in the drying rack. Pop liked him to dry them with a tea towel straight away, but if he put the washing on first, then they'd be nearly dry when he came back to them.

Tracy said, 'Why don't you put them in the dishwasher Tobe?'

'Pop and me, are the dish washers. It doesn't take long.' Toby wanted to point out Pop was a pensioner and money was scarce most of the time, but he held his tongue.

'God, I don't think I could live without ours, I even hate emptying it.' She winked at him and attempted a shiver to illustrate her point. 'The girls'll be fine in there for a while. I'll bring their iPads back and that'll entertain them today. Adele'll get sick of ABC Kids soon enough, so let them watch the Disney channel, that always keeps them busy. Anyway, I'm counting on you to keep them occupied till then. Reckon you can do that?'

Toby shrugged. 'Ugh, we don't have pay TV either... Sorry.'

'Well no worries, you'll think of something I'm sure. By the way, they're only allowed bottled water or juice. I don't like them drinking dairy or soft drinks and no butter on their sandwiches, okay. Good lad. I put our clothes in the laundry, and if you can, do my smalls on a gentle wash and in cold water. Hang them in the shower for me, and I'll fold them later.'

He couldn't believe it. iPads, pay TV, bottled water. They spoiled these kids, more than they could know. Tracy was saying goodbye to her daughters one last time, and telling them that Toby was in charge until she got back.

When the dishes were done, he started toward the laundry when he felt her hand on his shoulder.

'Pop's done a good job with you, Tobe.' He felt her lips stick to his skin when she kissed his cheek. 'You're turning out alright.'

'Ta.' He turned away, he wasn't used to a woman's attention and conflicting thoughts scrambled his mind. 'I have to get this under control.' Toby was sure the words were only thoughts, but no, he had said them out loud. Quiet, but loud enough for Tracy to hear.

'Sure you do...' She giggled, and hurried out.

'The washing...' Toby's words trailed after her. Embarrassment began to crush him and he thought of things he could say to hide it, but the words wouldn't come. He diverted his mind by thinking about Shamus.

If Pop wanted to put bunks in the study, then the desk had to go into Toby's room. He knew it would be hard to find space and it was heavy. If he got an old blanket from the shed, he could put it on that and drag it along the carpet. He started removing the drawers and carrying them to his room. Where were his mates? They could keep the kids entertained while he did this.

'What are you doing?' Jasmin startled him.

Before Toby could answer, Adele said, 'He's moving his stuff, so we can sleep in this room.'

'Tell you what,' Toby said. 'If you can carry these stacks of papers and stuff onto my bed we'll soon be finished.'

Jazz didn't move. 'What do we get?' she said.

'What do you mean, what do you get?' Toby said.

'Well, when we help at home, Mum pays us five dollars.' Jazz had her hands on her hips, her head cocked sideways.

'Shush Jazzy. Mum said you weren't to say stuff like that to Toby.'

'What, you kids get paid to do chores? How much?' Toby felt his temper rising. It was obvious their parents spoiled them.

'Five dollars, sometimes more. We save it in our piggy banks for when we go on holiday,' turning away, Adele pointed her toes inward and looked at the ground, 'we're allowed to spend it on rides and stuff.'

Jasmin smirked. 'Except, when we went to Hawaii last year, Dad paid for everything. We even went to Disneyland when I was three. Have you ever been to Disneyland, Toby? You should go, shouldn't he, Adele?'

'One day, maybe, when I'm older.'

Adele leaned against the door frame; her eyes were still down. 'Toby, are you our brother?' She looked straight at him. 'Once I asked Mum and Dad what happened to my brother and they told me he had died, but you're not dead, are you? You came to live with Pop, didn't you?' She stared at him. 'I remember, I was almost four and you were nine. That's right, isn't it? You're my big brother, aren't you?'

Adele reached out and held his face in her hands. She looked directly at him. 'Why did you leave me, Toby?

Was it something I did? Did you have to go away because we needed your room for Jazzy?'

He pushed her hands from his face. 'Your Mum will have to answer that. I don't know what she's told you, or why you'd think I'm your brother.' Toby choked on the words and picked up another drawer. 'Come on you two. I'll pay you with a story.'

Adele was not going to let it rest. 'Okay, but tell me the one about the boy who was bad. You know the one, his parents sent him to live with the old grandfather, and they never heard from him ever again.'

'Only when we're finished.'

'Deal.' Adele said spat in her right palm and put it out for Toby to shake. Jazzy followed her lead.

Toby bemused by their ritual, shook their hands. 'Deal done, then.'

'Spit seals the deal... Argh!' Jazz said, 'it's what pirates do,'

A horn sounded in the street. The girls pushed ahead to see who was there and Toby welcomed their distraction. They watched a white van beeping its way down the drive and stopping near the back of the house. The driver slid down from the seat, when his feet hit the ground, his tummy, big and hairy, jiggled under his too short fluoro singlet.

Embroidered with black and red, Quick-Az Couriers, contrasted against the bright yellow fabric. His steps were short, and Toby thought his boots were too large for him. He wore a red bandanna covered with white Canteen emblems. His navy shorts hung low and you could see the band of his underpants. It was grey. *That's what you get when you don't separate your washing.*

'Arthur Farrier's place?' The mouth below the yard broom on his top lip hardly moved.

'Sorry, yeah.' Toby said pushing the girls back onto the porch. 'Arthur Farrier lives here,'

'I got a delivery for him. Is he here?'

'Not at the moment,' Toby said. 'But I can sign for him. What is it?'

'Dunno kid, it's all boxes and dead weight to me. Anyone here to give me a hand?'

Toby held his hands wide. 'Just me.'

'That's lovely, they always do this to me,' The driver said opening the back doors of the van.

The girls were laughing, his bum jiggled sideways with each step and they thought he'd lose his shorts at any time. A wave vibrated from his loose-fitting boots all the way to his shoulders, and he puffed like a steam train. They whispered loudly about his curly black hair, his fat legs, then giggled more.

Toby shot them a look hot enough to peel paint. 'Into the house both of you,' Toby shouted to them. 'I'll talk to you later.'

'Sorry about that,' he said.

'Don't worry about it kid, I know I'm hairy, fat and fifty, but the missus loves me and that's all that matters.' He gave Toby a box. 'Here you take the smalls and I'll get the big stuff.'

'A Wii?'

'Yep, someone's had a big spend up. The people to install it should be here about one, or at least that's what they told me.'

'A Wii. He bought a Wii.'

'Yep, come on kid, the name on the shirt says quick as, but if we dawdle around here much more we'll hafta get all the signs changed to *Maybe Tomorrow*.' He laughed at his own joke. 'Here's a Play station too.

You've hit the jackpot young fella. Glad I don't have to hook it all up. Bit dumb with electrics me.'

At the end of unloading, Toby thought Pop had gone mad, or maybe it was Tracy. Yeah that had to be it, Pop would never spend money like that. Manny the Vanny, as the driver called himself, insisted every item be accounted for.

'Never too early to learn this stuff, kid. Not every driver is up to snuff.' He tapped his nose. 'Know what I mean.'

Toby checked the manifest again, signed it and handed it back. 'Yeah thanks Manny, and I'm sorry about before. The girls were outta line.'

'Don't worry kid, I can't be offended by people who don't know me. You're alright...?'

'Toby, my name's Toby.'

'Like I said, you're alright Toby. Take care and don't be too hard on them young-uns, you hear me now.'

'I'll tell them a story about the rude kids and the nice van driver, yeah?'

'You do that.' Manny laughed all the way to the driver's door. He looked at his running sheet and swung up behind the wheel. A wave of his hairy right arm and Manny the vanny disappeared.

Toby stormed into the lounge room. 'Okay you two, because you were rude, you can tidy up in here right now. Get all those toys back into your cases. We've got work to do.'

'But we're playing.' Jazzy pouted, crossed her arms and stomped her foot.

'Not anymore. I've had it watching you two not doing anything, and me running around trying to keep you happy. Toby let anger creep into his voice. He wasn't jealous of his sisters, more amazed at how lazy and spoiled they were. 'Hop to it now.' He bent down and turned off the TV. 'Let me know when you are done. I'll give you five minutes.'

'How about ten?' Adele asked.

'Five, and if there is anything on the floor when I come back, it goes in the bin, understand.'

Jazz scowled. 'You're not the boss of us.'

'I am today. Now get on with it. You've got five minutes that's all.'

Toby had squeezed the desk and the filing cabinet into his room. The girls carried a few small boxes into the lounge room and put them in the corner he had directed them too.

Jasmine tugged at his tee shirt. 'I'm hungry. Is it lunch yet?'

'Mum says you're not to ask for food.' Adele frowned at her sister and crossed her arms. 'It's not twelve yet, and we always have lunch at twelve, you know that.'

'Have an apple,' Toby said. 'I have to get this washing out.'

'She doesn't like apples.'

'There are carrots in the crisper at the bottom of the fridge. Eat one of them.'

'I don't like carrot.' Jasmine's whine was beginning to grate.

'Go without until lunch then. I've got things to do.'

Another van slowed in the street and reversed into their driveway. The driver rolled the back door of his vehicle up. More boxes Toby thought.

'This the Farrier place?'

'Says so on the letterbox.' Toby didn't want to get smart, but somehow that's the way it was going today.

'No need to be clever, kid. I've got a delivery that's all.'

'Yeah, I know. I'm sorry Sir.'

'Okay, any adults around to get this stuff outta the truck, I did me back yesterday and I'm not supposed to lift.'

'Just me.'

'Ah well, you'll have to do it then.'

'But, it's your job, isn't it?'

'Yeah, but I've done me back see, and I'm late already. Put the washing down and fly up in the back there, that's a good lad. I'll tell you what you need to do. No sweat, no pack-drill.' The driver was cheerful. 'Here, I'll come up and untie things, you walk 'em to the edge of the doorway, then lean 'em back and slide 'em down, easy-peasy.' The driver had a singsong sound, and the rhythm in his voice timed with the way he instructed Toby to do things. 'Now lad, jump down and use the trolley to take 'em to where they have to go. No point double handling.'

'What are they?'

'Hang on.' He checked the manifest. 'A bunk set and a couple of mattresses.'

'All new?' Toby said.

'Yep, looks like you won the lottery, kid.'

'The room's not ready yet, I've got to vacuum.'

'Leave them on the veranda then. I'd reckon you should unpack it all out here first and assemble it when you get it inside.'

Toby worked the mattresses down as instructed and took particular notice of the way the driver had said to put them on the beds.

The driver held the clipboard out for Toby to sign and shut the truck's door. 'Just wack your John Henry on there fella, that's a good boy.'

Toby didn't appreciate the tone and felt his temper flare again. He took a deep breath. 'Says here, driver to assemble and remove packaging.' Much more of this and he could see himself really losing it.

'Yeah it always says that, but you'll be right. There's an allen key with the instructions. A clever kid like you will work it out.'

'Stuff that.' Toby threw the ball point on the ground. 'If it says you'll assemble and take the packaging, then that's what's gunna happen. Just because I'm a kid it doesn't mean I have to take your crap.'

The driver picked up his pen. 'What's your name boy?'

'Toby.'

He smiled and signed the docket with Toby's name. 'Gotcha kid.' He tore off the receipt and slapped it against Toby's chest before sauntering to the cabin and lifting himself into the seat. 'Let that be a lesson boy. Don't piss off the big dogs.'

'What's going on here?'

Toby looked past the van to see the two police officers standing in front of it. Jenny Azzopardi had parked the police car across the driveway.

'Trouble?' Constable John Evans stood between the gate and Toby.

Toby passed John the paperwork. 'The cartnote says that it includes assembly and disposal of the packaging. I was pointing that out when the driver signed my name on it, and jumped in his truck.'

'Bit of fraud and a breach of contract here I think, Jenny.' John slapped the side of the van. 'Reckon we should get traffic down for a look over his truck?'

'Better than that, we're on a roll today, how about we check for warrants and look into his history while we're at it?' She smiled at the driver. 'We don't like bullies, do we, John?'

'Righto, mate. That'll take Constable Azzopardi some time, so now you have a few hours to do what it said on the invoice. I'd get a move on if I were you.'

'He's got a bad back,' Toby said.

'Not with those guns,' Jenny said. 'Did you get the kid to help you unload?'

'I told him what to do, yeah,' he answered.

Jenny smiled at him, 'Oh boy, you're gunna wish you hadn't done that,' she said.

John looked at the washing. 'Come on Tobe, I'll help you hang this lot out.' He turned back to the driver. 'Well, get on with it then and no short cuts, I'll be checking your work.'

While they made lunch for the girls, John and Toby talked. It was just bloke stuff, but Toby felt his spirits lift. The policeman said nothing about the assault, the desk, or his family.

The van driver heaved card board boxes into the truck as if they were paper, and his cursing had drawn admonishment from Jenny more than once.

He knocked on the back door. 'All finished out here, if you give me a hand we can carry them in.'

'Yeah sure,' John said. 'Coming now. Is the room ready, Tobe?'

'Good enough, I'll tidy it after.'

'What did you find out?' the driver asked Jenny.

'Oh, I just sat here and did a couple of reports. I didn't have time to worry about you. But I have put your name in our complaints database, so you'd better keep your nose clean, eh?'

'You bitch,' he whispered.

Jenny grinned. 'You betcha.' She followed him out. 'I'll just shift the car for you.

Toby shifted on his feet as he felt John study him. The policeman opened and shut his mouth a couple of times, then said, 'Come out away from the girls, mate.' They went to the shed and he asked, 'Where is everybody?'

'Tracy is off to her insurance brokers, and I don't know when she'll be back. Pop? Well look around. This isn't like him to blow money on new stuff. I mean everything I've ever had is second hand. Look, I'm going to have to get these beds made up and then there's someone coming to install all of this.' He pointed to the flat-screen television and a row of sound system boxes. 'There's a small fortune here, and it's all because of them.' He nodded toward the door.

'You feeling jealous, or a bit hard done by, maybe?'

'I'm not jealous, but yeah. Where was all this when I was growing up?'

'I can't answer that, mate, but maybe he's trying to give them, in material stuff, what he gave you in life.' John put his arm around Toby's shoulder. 'He lost his family back then. Maybe he wants it put right again and at the moment, this is the only way he knows how.'

'Yeah, I suppose, but the girls are so spoiled.'

'But can they do the stuff you can do?' He pushed Toby off balance and caught him again. 'Toby Farrier, Australia's Best Selling Author. Can they do that?' John Evans grinned and Toby couldn't help but smile back. 'That's better. Now Jen and me would like to take a look at this book that's causing all this grief, is that okay with you?'

'Yeah, but it's not here,' Toby said.

'Did the bloke from yesterday pinch it?'

'Nope, I hid it.'

'Where?' John rubbed his head in thought.

'In the old book section of the State Library, but you'll never find it, I'll have to show you.'

John laughed. 'You're one clever kid Toby Farrier, and never let anyone make you think different, okay. One more thing, the sketch and description in the book you gave Danny Sabo. Is he the bloke from yesterday afternoon?'

'Yeah.'

'Have you ever seen him before?'

'Only when he slapped my hand at the library, and when I was coming through the fence.'

And the bloke who attacked Sophia last night, do you know who he is?'

'Not quite sure, do you?'

'We have an idea, but I'm keen to hear your thoughts about him.'

'I reckon it's the same bloke, the History Professor that Willy sent some photos to, Phillip Ryan. How dangerous do you reckon he is?'

'Sophia seems to think so too,' John didn't want to alarm Toby any more than necessary, so ignored his question, 'and she's worried about you.'

'Is she alright?'

'She'll need a couple of days. She's stiff and sore today though. Give her a call when you can, eh.'

'Sure,' Toby shrugged and wondered when he'd find time. 'it'll be later though.'

Constable Azzopardi joined them. 'Can we keep the ledger for a bit, I want to take a photocopy of your sketch? It was a smart move to log a date and time on it too. Well done,' she said. 'Reckon we'd better leave you to it, Toby. John and I have a crook to catch.' She smiled and shook his hand. 'You have a couple of cute sisters too.'

'They're okay, but I'd better clean up their lunch mess before Pop gets back.'

CHAPTER THIRTY-FOUR

Toby was folding the washing into the wicker basket when the shadow of something coming from behind startled him. He spun around to face a woman a size bigger and a touch older than Tracy.

'Wow, I need one of them,' the woman said, she was wearing the same corporate shirt as Manny, only hers was pressed and without the stains where beetroot had landed.

'It was my Nan's. Pop's had it for years.'

'Nah, not the basket mate. I meant a bloke who can fold washing.' She laughed and held out her hand. 'I'm Larissa, we're here to install the television and sound system, she pointed to the boxes on the porch. Is this all of it?' Her words came fast and business like. 'Did Manny tell you what time we'd be here?'

'He just said later today.'

'Good,' her speech slowing and to Toby she seemed to relax, 'it's just that we've been held up installing an alarm system, that's all. Show me where, and I'll make a start.'

Toby took her into the lounge, where it was still a mess, the girls had scattered Lego all over the place. 'What did I say? Come on you two, tidy this up now. This lady is here to set up a new television and a Wii.'

They looked at Toby. 'You help us too,' Jasmine said.

'Anything I pick up goes in the bin, I told you that before. Now you have five minutes. Put the toys in your room. Then I'll come in and tell you all about Toby and the pirate princesses.' They didn't move. 'Hop to it...' he clapped his hands. 'Now!'

Toby went outside to the porch and helped the technicians with opening and unpacking the boxes. He could hear the girls arguing about the Lego, but at least they were doing it.

Arthur came home and asked where the girls were. Toby nodded to the door. He heard their squeals when they saw Arthur. He heard Arthur offer to help them clean up. He shook his head. They'll never learn unless they do it themselves. His grandfather was so different with the girls than he had been when he had come here to live. Adele said his name and that he'd threatened to throw the Lego away. He cringed at the accusation, but stopped himself from going in there to explain. He listened harder.

'Oh well, I suppose he was too busy to do it,' Arthur said

'Nope, he was just talking to the police. I think he's in trouble,' Jasmine said. 'They asked him lots of questions.'

Toby scowled. *Why did they always think he was in trouble?*

'I don't think we'll worry too much about all that now, Jazz. How about you, Adele, did you get lunch?' Pop asked.

'Yeah, Mum doesn't like us eating white bread or fatty sausage, but it was okay I guess,' Adele said. 'Toby's been busy all day, he told us to tidy up so the TV lady could do her stuff. I don't think he really would have thrown our stuff out. Jazzy is a bit of a dobber sometimes.'

Toby smiled. He was growing to like Adele. Jasmine on the other hand...

'Well, you're dobbing now,' Jasmine said.

The door banged and Arthur came out. Toby nodded to him and he nodded back.

'Mr Farrier?' the woman said.

'That's me,' Arthur said offering his hand.

She shook it, 'where do you want the security cameras mounted,'

'Good grief, I haven't thought this through. Toby'll work it out with you.'

'Whenever you're ready, mate,' she said.

'Yes, yes.' Arthur frowned. 'Tobe, I'm going to catch Charlie before he sees his doctor.'

Ben sauntered into the yard and waved. 'Toby, Mr Farrier.'

Nathan was a step behind him. 'We just come around to see how our man is today. Hear you had a bit of trouble yesterday fella.'

'Yeah a bit.' Toby shook hands with his friends.

'Look boys,' Arthur said. 'You'd better push off, Toby has his sisters here today, and he's got chores at the moment. Maybe tomorrow, yeah?'

'Pop?' Toby drew the word out.

'No, Toby, you're too busy to skive off with your mates. Sorry boys, but you'd better go.'

One of the techs called from inside. 'We're going to need a bit of help in here.'

Nathan called back. 'Coming,' he winked at Arthur. 'Just help out in here first, shall I?'

'Go on then, you scheming pack of devils. No getting in anybody's way though, understand?' Arthur smiled and tapped Toby on the shoulder. 'If I'm not back by four o'clock, you'd better put that roast lamb on. Do plenty of vegies because there'll be six of us, Charlie's coming too.'

Another job Toby thought, but he smiled at his grandfather. 'Good as done, Pop.'

Toby slumped on the corner of the entertainment unit.

'Are you supposed to sit on that?' Jack fist pumped Toby.

'I really don't care much at the moment. I got the mud belted out of me yesterday. Soph gets attacked in the park, my long-lost stepmother has dropped my sisters on me, and Pop is off spending money like he's won the lottery or something. Oh, and my dad's in a coma.'

'I hate to break it to you like this pal, but your pop did win the lottery, remember?' Ben slapped his friend's back. 'So, he's got a few bucks to splash around now and he wants to spoil you a bit, that's all. You have to chill a bit Tobe old mate. Things are sweet now.'

Toby started to let himself in on the joke, but to keep Ben on his feet, he pouted. 'Doesn't explain why he's treating me like his slave though.'

'We sold you to him, idiot. You are his slave now, man...' Jack laughed. 'We heard about Soph and called in before we come here. She's sore, but okay. Her dad says you took the bloke on.'

Nathan clasped his hands in front of his chest, tilted his head and swayed. 'You're her hero.'

'Yeah, right.' Toby wanted this to stop.

Ben reached out and touched Toby's zit. 'Welcome to the club mate. We were all taking bets that you'd get through school without that.'

Toby flinched.

'Bit tender too. Well we all know how that feels. Come on, Tobe. Tell us what to do so we can get this play station hooked up.'

CHAPTER THIRTY-FIVE

Ben shook the doona into the corners of its cover. 'New doonas, latex pillows and everything a little girl could need, yeah?'

'Craps me off a bit though, and I know it shouldn't.' Toby waved his arms around the room. 'Yesterday this was mine, and now it's gone.' He checked the new bedside clock. 'Time to start tea, you want to peel some spuds?'

'Sure,' Ben said. 'I know it's gunna be rough for the next couple of days, but your Pop thinks more of you than anyone. You know that.'

'You reckon? He's not showing it much today.'

'Look Tobe, who else can he dump all of this on, and know it'll get done. My mum says you can only hurt the ones you care about. Well I know Arthur cares about you. Look around, most of your friends would kill to get on with their pop like you do. It's just one of the things that makes me and the boys envious.' He shoved Toby's shoulder. 'Why do you think we hang around you, mate? It's all about Arthur and Charlie for us.' He was laughing. 'Come on, teach me to cook, and maybe I'll surprise Mum with dinner one night.'

The house was still buzzing with technical people when Tracy walked into the kitchen. 'Smells good,' she said as she looked in the pots on the stove. 'What's with all the tradies, Tobe?'

'Pop's had a big spend up. Wants to make the place a bit more comfortable, I think.'

'The girls been good?'

'Yeah, I made them pick up their Lego, they didn't like it much, but did it anyway.' He pointed at the passage. 'They're up in Pop's room. My mates Nathan and Jack are supposed to be reading to them, but by those laughs, I think Jack might be doing his rubbery face routine.' He grinned, and a sense of pride washed over him, he savoured it. It felt good to know he'd managed the day. 'Sorry, Tracy, this is my mate, Ben. Ben this is Tracy my step—'

'Hi Ben, pleased to meet you. I'm Tracy, Toby's mum. I'll go and introduce myself to the rest of your gang.'

She kissed Toby on the cheek. 'There are some bags and stuff I've left in the back of the car, bring it in when you have a minute. The groceries leave here and everything else you can put in my room.' She walked toward the giggling.

'Wow, she's nice,' Ben said. 'And she looks like someone off the front of a fashion magazine.'

'I guess.' Toby looked down and hung up the tea towel.

'You guess?' Ben's eyes followed her until she reached the end of the passage. 'I wish my mum looked like that. In fact, I bet my mum, wishes she looked like that.' Ben hung his arm over Toby's shoulder. 'Come on mate, let's bring her stuff in.'

Jack and Nathan soon joined them at the back of the four-wheel drive, they were muttering and giggling. All Toby wanted to do was hide in his room, one request from Tracy, and his mates were falling over themselves to help.

'Grow up you lot, she's just my stepmother. We'd better get this inside like she said.'

'Sorry, Toby, but she is...' Jack shook his fingers, '...tsss, hot.'

'Go home you lot. I can get this.' He snatched a bag from Nathan's hand.

'Come on Toby, we'll help you in with it, and then we'll go, alright?' Ben said. 'You blokes get that lot inside, and I'll help Toby finish out here.' He loaded Jack and Nathan and ushered them off.

'I know they don't mean much, but it's hard,' Toby said.

'Yeah mate, I know too.' He patted Toby's back. 'I'll settle them down, but one day you'll have to tell us everything about the young Toby Farrier. All of it and from the beginning too. How it was that he came to live with his pop and not stay with his mum and dad.'

'Someday,' Toby said staring at his shoes, 'someday soon.'

The trades people left soon after his mates. Tracy had bathed the girls and was in the lounge flipping through the television channels. A monitor in the kitchen scrolled images of the street, the driveway, the lane and the back yard. Toby thought the whole thing was overkill. What was Pop thinking? They didn't need all this stuff. His sisters could read books, play games and talk to each other, just as he'd done. Being alone without all the gizmos had fired his imagination and made him want to write. His sisters deserved that too.

He grabbed what he needed from the cutlery drawer, began setting the table and looking up at the photo of his grandmother asked, 'what do you make of it all, Nan?' A hand caressed his shoulder. He spun around to see Tracy there.

'Did you ask me something, Tobe?' Tracy asked.

'No, I was just thinking out loud.' He took the picture of his grandmother from the mantle and looked at it. 'I wondered what she would have made of Pop's big buy up today. He'd have spent ten grand I reckon, maybe more.'

'From what I've heard Lois would have cautioned care, but gone along with it anyway.'

'Did you see Dad?'

'Called in after the insurers, no change I'm afraid.' She turned away and dabbed her eyes with a tissue she dragged from the box on the sideboard. 'I have to believe he'll pull through; I might look like I'm in charge, but inside I'm frightened. You know when I told you I needed to suit up; well I've had to do that all my life. Pretend to be tough, just to keep up with my friends.' She took the picture from Toby and kissed it. 'Now Lois here, she didn't have to do that. Darren told me she was one tough lady. Often had to go to the school and pull him out of trouble. She frightened his teachers, anyway.' She put the photo back. 'Bless you Lois, he turned out a good man.'

'Who Dad?'

'Bit of a handful, he said, always had detention. He must have been kinda wild as a kid.' Her hands cupped Toby's face. 'Tore this place up once or twice too, but she put a stop to that.'

'Wow.'

'You two have a lot of catching up to do, when your dad comes out of his coma. The doctors have him stabilised now, and when the swelling goes down, they'll set his leg and arm'

'While he's out to it?'

'So, they say.'

Charlie and Arthur stumbled through the door. The whiff of alcohol trailing them like a faithful dog.

'How's tea going, Tobe, everything under control,' Arthur asked, swaying in the kitchen doorway.

'Sure Pop. Twenty minutes.' Toby smiled at him. 'Are you okay, or has Mr Rankin been twisting your arm again?'

Arthur waddled his way toward the lounge with his hand in the air. 'Don't you worry about me.'

'He'll be okay, Tobe, but he's had a big day,' Charlie said. 'I'll take him through. Just give us a call when you're ready, eh.' Charlie didn't sway as much as Arthur, but the smell of grog gave him away too.

'Will do, but I've never seen him like this? Well not this drunk anyway.'

'Tobe, it's twenty years today since your nan passed away, and I think with Tracy, the kids, and Darren in hospital it's all been a bit much. He'll have a headache tomorrow, but he'll be okay.' Charlie sat on the corner stool. 'He loves you mate.'

'I know, it's just...'

'Yeah, I do know. How about I give you a hand, while them in there get more acquainted.'

'You want to carve?' Toby said and passed the knife.

'Have you let it rest?'

'Yep, just like they said on the telly, I took it out ten minutes ago, got the greens and the gravy to do. If you carve, I'll dish up.'

Charlie's eyes lit up. 'He, who carves, gets the shank.'

'The rules according to Arthur,' Toby said and he felt his load lighten.

Charlie drew an exaggerated breath through his nostrils, closed his eyes and smiled. He nudged Toby and said, 'I gave up a date with Nichole Kidman for this. Just like they used to say on that old ad on TV.'

Toby pictured him with the shank, all soft, gooey, gelatinous and sticking to his fingers. Juice would soon be streaming down his chin. 'Come on, as Pop would say, let's get 'em fed, and into bed.'

Charlie carried two plates on each arm. 'Practice, Toby, practice. Too many years ago to remember, I'd wait tables for pocket money. Some things you don't forget. Or did I tell you that, once before.'

'Can't say you did,' Toby lied. He winked and let a broad smile cross his face.

'Grub's up.' Charlie declared as he put the plates down, and held the chair out for Tracy. 'I guess you must be Miss Tracy, the big sister of these lovely young ladies.'

'Why thank you Mr Rankin, Sir.' Tracy exaggerated her curtsey with a deep flourish. 'You are far too kind.'

'A pleasure to have the company of three beautiful young women tonight, I'm sure.' He winked at Adele and Jasmine. 'Shall we dine?' He helped push Tracy's chair in and after the girls sat down, Charlie lowered into his.

'Dig in kids,' Arthur said, 'I know if your Nan were with us now, she wouldn't want you to wait.' He blew a kiss to the photo of Lois. 'Love of my life that woman, the love of my life.' A tear rolled out of the corner of his eye.

Toby knew Pop could become maudlin at times, but tonight was different. He wasn't sure if it was the booze, Darren's accident, or Tracy and the girls being there, but Pop had a peaceful kind of melancholy about him.

'You had a good day, little one?' Pop pointed his fork at Jasmine, a glob of gravy and roast potato fell back into the gravy on his plate. 'Oops.'

'Kinda,' she said. 'Toby's friends were nice, at least they didn't yell at me.'

'Who yelled at you?' Arthur asked.

'He did.' She pointed her knife at Toby. 'And, he didn't keep his promise.'

'Jasmine Elizabeth Farrier.' Tracy raised her voice. 'Are you telling tales?'

Adele leapt in. 'She always dobs, Mum, you know she does.'

'He did yell at me. I promise Mum, he did.'

Adele clattered her fork onto the plate. 'He yelled at both of us, well not really yelled. He told us to pack up the toys because people were trying to set up the television.'

Jazz didn't want to let it rest. 'He said he'd throw our toys in the rubbish.'

'Not nice Toby, these are your sisters. You can't go around threatening them like that. They are only little and don't understand.' Arthur pointed at Jasmine and said, 'I'll make sure Toby doesn't do it again, okay?'

Jasmine stared at Toby and grinned.

After dinner and helping get Arthur into bed, Charlie came into the kitchen where Toby again had his hands in the sink. Putting a hand on his young friend's shoulder he said, 'Might be an idea if you stay home tonight and look after the girls for Tracy. I know it's not what you wanted, but you'll see your dad when he wakes up.'

'You think Dad's going to be okay?'

'I dunno mate, but if prayer has anything to do with it he will. I've never heard that old Pop of yours bother God, as much as he has in the last twenty-four hours.'

'I didn't know Pop was a believer.'

'Yep, your Nan and him, at Mass every week.' Charlie took down a picture of Arthur and Toby from the mantelpiece. 'Stopped believing for a bit after she died, started again when you came to live. Tobe, he loves you, and as much as he did her. You'll have to forgive Artie a bit at the moment he's got a lot going on right now.'

'I know, but people forget it's happening to me too.' Toby looked at Charlie, hoping he'd say something prophetic. 'Do you think I'm in danger?'

Charlie bumped his palm to his forehead. 'Jeez son, I completely forgot about that. I can't say that you're as completely safe as I'd like to. But I do think the immediate danger is past though. This bloke is hurt and on the run. In all the books, I've read, these creeps go to ground and lick their wounds for a while. I reckon that's what this bloke'll do.' Charlie pushed his glasses back to the bridge of his nose. 'And didn't the copper John say they'd send a patrol past once in a while?'

Toby looked at him. 'Is what you read fiction or fact?'

'Probably fiction based on fact.' Charlie laughed. 'All bulldust probably, sorry, Tobe.'

'I thought so, but thanks for making me laugh.' Toby put an arm around his companion. 'You've always been here for me too. I wouldn't have straightened out without you and Pop. There's a chance I'd be worse than Slash. You blokes gave me a dream to follow when I didn't have one. I'll never be able to repay that.' Charlie picked up a tissue, but Toby had him off guard and slopped the dish mop on his cheek, suds hung from his whiskers. 'Not a word to Pop about me getting worked up now, promise? Like you said he has a lot going on.'

'You're a good kid, Toby.' Charlie said.

Toby turned to wipe the stovetop.

'You're all soapy too, now.'

Toby turned back to see what Charlie meant, his face met a hand full of bubbles.

'I used to get Elsie every time with that one.' He laughed. 'Had so much soap on her face over the years, she took up shaving.' He pulled a face and dragged an imaginary razor down his cheek.

'And I imagine she'd rip right into you too, if she was here to see you now.'

'You're right, Tobe, exactly right, but we'd laugh about it and until late too. She loved a joke, my Elsie.' Charlie hung the tea towel over the rail. 'I better be off now. Take good care of them mate, they need you now. All of them.'

With Tracy at the hospital and the girls asleep, Toby went to check on his grandfather. Hearing Arthur snore, a picture played in his mind. He imagined the walls expanding and contracting, in time to the old man's noise. He placed a glass of water on the side table with a couple of Aspirin. Pop would need those through the night, he always did.

Toby lay on his bed. He couldn't stop thinking about the attack at the tram stop, and his dad's accident. It kept whirring through his head. His thoughts were odd and painful. Ideas darted around at the back of his mind like marbles in a jam tin, each one there for a moment and then replaced by another. He needed to focus, so he counted the ribs in the tongue and groove ceiling. It had helped him rest before, but not tonight. All he could do was write the events down, and make a story out of them.

His fingers touched the damage wrought by their burglar, and whispered as if the desk could hear him. 'I'll find the bloke who did this.' He rolled the top back and sat down. 'We'll have plenty of adventures to share with anyone who'll read our stories... But first you have to help me find whatever it was that Shamus was working on.' Toby knew the desk was inanimate, but talking to it offered comfort.

CHAPTER THIRTY-SIX

Toby heard a car door close in the driveway. The display on his alarm showed it was a bit after one. Although he'd drifted in and out of sleep for the past couple of hours, his senses flicked to alert. He lay there wondering if the burglar was back and his fingers felt under his bed for the handle of a golf club. He could feel his heart race and now even his breath caught in his throat, but he was ready. No harm would come to anyone staying in this house tonight.

In the shadow of his bedroom door, he opened and closed his hands on the leather grip of Arthur's number three wood. Against the slumber of the city, fast footsteps in the driveway rattled in his ears. He heard them on the back veranda and a key slide into the lock. The squeak from the back door grated, he sniffed, perfume floated on the air, and relief overtook him, it was Tracy. He slid his weapon back under the bed.

'You still up, mate?' Tracy whispered, and squeezed through the opening of his half-shut door.

Toby sat on the edge of his bed and turned on the lamp. 'Yeah with all that's happened this week, I couldn't sleep.' He kicked at the handle of the stick forcing it further under the bed.

She smiled at him. 'Was that...' Tracy put a hand over her mouth. 'Did you think I was breaking in?'

'I wasn't sure? I heard a car door and footsteps. When the back door opened and I smelt your perfume I knew it was you.' Toby tugged at his boxer shorts and smoothed them around his thighs. 'J-Adore, I think you said it was, anyway that's when I knew it was you.' Tracy made him feel at ease, and whenever he thought back to his childhood, he could only remember the good stuff. He was sure she disciplined him, but couldn't remember her being spiteful.

'Maybe it is my invisible force field?' She laughed. 'I wish I'd sprayed some on your dad's truck before he left. Mind if I sit down, I know it's late, but we haven't had much of a catch up, have we?'

'I'll move up a bit.' Toby stood up, ran his thumbs around the elastic waist of his boxers and clutching his pillow to his chest sat down again. 'I guess with what's happened to Dad, Pop and Charlie winning second division in the lottery and all, there hasn't been a lot of opportunity.' Toby could feel exhaustion in his words. He wanted to tell her that he felt everyone seemed to overlook his problems, but he held back.

'You know mate, it's not your job to look after everyone. I should know that more than anybody. It's because you just get on with things, we forget about how much you had going on, what with that bloke attacking you and all.'

'I...'

Tracy put a finger to his lips. 'You know John Evans came to see me and Darren tonight. He let me in on what happened just before I dumped all this on you at the hospital. Only then, did I learn how much stuff you've had going on, and I think I've been a bit unfair.'

'It's okay...' Toby squeezed his hands tight into the pillow.

'Tobe, I need to say this, please.' She squared her shoulders. 'For too long, Darren and I have tried to put what we did to one side. Trying not to remember how we failed you, we... I didn't understand how much we needed your forgiveness.' She reached across and patted his knee. 'Still do.' Tears stream down her cheeks. 'You know, everyone sees me, as this hardnosed business woman, someone without feelings. Yet every day, the little girl inside me wants to hide until a good fairy comes along and makes everything right.'

She dug around in her handbag and produced a long-haul driver's Log Book. 'This is your dad's. The day you left he started folding the pages a different way. Most truckies fold forward, but your dad turned them back. You might wonder why, but I think you'll find the answer in there somewhere. I know I did.' She passed it to him.

Toby ran his hand over the cover.

'You know, Terri, John Evan's sister, your mum Shellie, and me. We were all mates, right through school. When Michelle contracted breast cancer it was just the pits, and we all cried for days. When she found out she was having you, she was over the moon until they told her the therapy would harm your chance of survival. She told them she'd go full term and then have the treatment. She was so brave and so strong willed, Toby.' Tracy reached for a tissue blew her nose and struggled with her words. 'We couldn't talk her out of it.'

Toby wanted her to stop talking, he didn't want this now and felt it beginning to swamp him, but knew he needed to hear it.

'Maybe you remember the perfume because your mum wore it too, we all did. Darren gave it to us for being her bridesmaids.'

Toby picked up a box of tissues and passed them to his stepmother.

Tracy tried to laugh. 'You should hate us for what we did, and yet here you are passing me bloody tissues.'

'Pop taught me that holding a grudge is hard work and I reckon he's right.' He turned away, he didn't need tears and if he looked at Tracy, he knew they would empty the box in a minute. 'I was angry, and my moods made me quite a handful for a long time, but Pop never pressured me. Sure, I had to go to a new school, but nobody there knew how bad I was, and some of the kids had even more problems.'

'Yeah?' Tracy took the tissue box from him.

'I soon saw how lucky I was, to have someone who loved me as much as Pop did. I couldn't say it like this at the time, but I knew what I wanted to say. I just couldn't make the words come out. When I looked at what the teachers wrote on the whiteboard, everything looked like alphabet soup, letters everywhere.' Toby grabbed another tissue.

'We didn't know...' Tracy frowned.

'Charlie got me sorted. He told Pop he'd heard someone talking about ADHD and disruptive kids and how they were often given the wrong diagnosis on the radio. One appointment, and after a couple of hours of watching Shrek through a machine, we walked out with a prescription for new glasses. In a few days, I could see how the letters formed words, and even numbers made sense.'

'Clever old you, eh?' Tracy laughed, but in a strained way. 'There was so much bitterness between Darren and his Dad, what could we do?'

Toby just shrugged.

'It's been a long day and I have to get some sleep. Toby, you have to forget about what we need, or what Arthur needs for a few days and do what you have to do. Help John find this bloke who's terrorising you.'

He felt her arm around his shoulders. 'Yep.'

'You may not be a man yet, but you're more than a boy too. You can do anything you decide to do, Toby Farrier. You've proved that.' She dropped her hand onto his knee and gave a squeeze. 'And you're a good looker too, for a Farrier.' She kissed his forehead and stood up.

'See you tomorrow.' She reached the door and turned back. 'I almost forgot, for the zit. Worked for me when I was your age.' She threw something to him.

Toby caught it and scanned the packaging. 'Thanks.'

Too tired to look at the entries in his dad's log book, he thumbed its pages, rolled over and drifted into sleep.

CHAPTER THIRTY-SEVEN

Toby stood at Sophia's door and knocked, even though he could see her through the screen.

Looking at him Sophia dropped her toast onto the plate. 'You could've phoned me.' She looked across the table to her mother, and then to the door. Mrs Nguyen stood up and left the kitchen.

'I wanted to, but...'

'No, Toby.' Sophia picked up her toast again and threw it into the sink. She slapped the table with her other hand, jerked up from her chair and it flew back, clattering its way across the room. Sophia's nostrils flared and spittle followed her words. 'If you'd been worried, if you'd cared just one tiny bit about me, you'd have found a way. I thought we were friends. No not friends, I thought we were more than that. That dirty old book and Shamus O'Toole mean more to you than I do. More than your Pop, or everyone. For pity's sake Toby, for all I know, that creep might have been trying to rape me.'

Mrs Nguyen burst through the door and glared at her daughter. Her eyes shifted to Toby. 'You better go. Sophia doesn't want to see you again. You've caused enough trouble.'

'But I wanted...'

Mrs Nguyen cut him off. 'You go now, Toby Farrier, and don't come here again. I don't want you talking to our Sophia again. You understand, Toby? Never again.' She held the door open and pointed for him to go. 'Outside, you go now.'

Toby felt the force of her words, as much as he heard them. He slumped his shoulders and wondering if it were possible to carry much more guilt, Sophia's mother's words loaded on even more. He felt her eyes burning into his back as he dragged his feet out of the driveway. Not wanting to go home, he headed for the city.

Sloping past the smokers gathered outside the hospital, Toby tried to keep his eyes down. He didn't mean to, but as he looked up his eyes fixed on a man in his late thirties. Toby had seen him before, and although he had skirted past him last time, the patient intrigued him. Who was he? Toby wanted to look away again, but couldn't. He was different to others in the area, his arms and legs tattooed to resemble snakeskin. Short cropped hair, the ginger strands showing flecks of grey that were in need of brushing. Toby memorised every detail. He didn't know what drew him to this bloke, but drawn he was.

Yellow stains on the fingers of his right hand indicated a nicotine dependence. The hospital wheelchair had a drip-stand and Toby supposed the bag of saline delivered a cocktail of fluid and drugs. Toe nails were curled, and outlined with colour of black tea. It could be dirt or ink, but lines matched the straps on his Havaianas, making the cadaver-like digits look like claws. Skinny and gaunt, with only a crumpled hospital gown to cover his jaundiced skin. His was a body barely held together by life.

'Hey kid?'

Toby, still in a daze jumped, the cadaver's voice snapping him back to attention.

'Yeah, you with the Essendon backpack.' His voice sounding like dry gravel struggled through his wheeze. 'Give us a hand will ya?'

Toby tried to avoid looking into his eyes, they were green, and for a moment Toby imagined they were lit from behind. He remembered seeing the same colour when sunlight shone through a wine bottle. 'Lasers.' He checked his thoughts; did he really say it out loud.

'Yep. Eyes of Ireland, my mum used to say.' The creature pointed to his face. A nail like the ones on his toes extended his finger and it beckoned Toby over.

'Name's Lizard, well not really, but it's kinda what I'm reduced to these days. Appropriate though don't you think?' His lips parted, his smile revealing a cavern behind a gate of yellow teeth. Toby moved closer and could smell decaying lungs on Lizard's breath.

'Toby... Toby Farrier.' He held his hand out.

'Better not shake with you, Toby Farrier. All the stuff they have me on has turned my skin to paper.' Lizard dragged a plastic cup from under the towel resting on his lap and spat in it.

Toby tried to turn away, but his eyes locked onto the cup, blood lined spittle coagulated in the bottom. He felt bile rise in his gullet and wanted to retch, as he imagined the taste of the cup's contents.

'Reckon I left half a lung in there yesterday, Toby.' He hawked another laugh, and when his coughing settled, said, 'Do us a favour old mate and wheel me up to the lifts.'

'Sorry, I have to be somewhere, my dad's in here.' Toby tried to excuse himself. but he knew it sounded weak.

'Call me Larry, Larry O'Toole.' He pointed to the ramp to take him inside. 'Just push me up there then, Toby. I'll make it to the lift on my own...Please?' Larry looked at him with a sorrowful pose.

Toby was sure the eyes would roll from their sockets and he'd be chasing them like lost marbles.

'The lifts, Toby, you can help me mate. You know you want to.'

'Sure I do, but only because your name is O'Toole, I have got to know an O'Toole lately and he's brought me nothing but trouble. Tell me where to and I'll get you back to your ward, but then I have to see my Dad.'

Lizard hawked again. 'You're a good kid, Toby. Here let's get a selfie together.' With his other hand, he pulled out a mobile phone from under the towel. 'Come on now lean in, we'll get the hospital sign in too.'

Toby closed in and could smell a Palmolive soap kind of clean about his new friend, and yet there was something else too, not rancid, but close. He screwed his nose up. Lizard saw it in the phone's screen.

'Yeah, I smell like death, Tobe, that's what it is. My body dies a little bit more every day, but it could be worse. I could have been run over by that bus yesterday.' He pointed to a bus heading up Gratton Street. 'Left the brakes off, and while I lit a ciggy the chair took off down the path. Lucky for me a copper caught the handles. All that happened was I ended up sprawled out over the tar like a dropped pizza. Good as gold now though. It was so funny I crapped myself.' He started coughing again, more gunk escaped his lungs, and the morning light caught a blood lined cord of spittle hanging between Lizard's lip and the cup. 'Come on kid, I have some stuff up in the room I want to show you.

Toby took the handles, turned the chair and headed for the lifts. He pressed the button to call it down when he realised he'd stopped thinking about himself. It felt good to let go for a while.

'O'Toole, eh, which one?' Lizard asked.

'An old one, from the twenties, a bloke called Shamus, he was some kind of policeman.' Toby checked himself. 'History project.'

'O'Tooles can be fun. C'mon hit the button to palliative care.'

CHAPTER THIRTY-EIGHT

The doors closed and Toby pulled the wheel chair into the back of the lift. Lizard pushed the button for his floor and they rode in silence. People stepped in and others got out, but nobody chose to look at them. Lizard muffled a few coughs into a handkerchief he clamped over his mouth. The doors opened.

'Here we are Toby. God's waiting room, or Satan's sundeck, depending on what you've done, and who you believe. Palliative Care, great people in here, but at the end of the day, only visitors and the staff go home.' Lizard motioned his arm about as if he owned the place. 'I was supposed to have gone out feet first a month ago, but damn it, I'm not ready yet.' He hacked, and another blob of bloodstained goo dribbled into his cup.

Toby swallowed hard, he didn't need to witness this. He had come to visit his father this morning, and after Sophia had balled him out, all he wanted to do was disappear for a while. 'I'd better get going I suppose.'

'No hurry on my account, Tobe. Ever seen a dead body?'

Toby stepped back. 'That's just gross.'

'Sit with me for a while, old Jock over there in the bed by the window.' He half lifted his hand and stretched his stained finger. 'Like me, no family. Lung cancer, cigarettes and asbestos they reckon, anyway old Jock's a dead man too. He's just hanging on here until he dies. He's had priests and parsons visit him, but waved them away, not a believer, he said. Do me a favour Toby go over and shake his hand, say hello and tell him your name. Just talk to him for a few minutes until I get back into bed.' Lizard winked and like the strobe from a lighthouse his eye flashed green. Larry wheeled toward the ensuite.

Toby could feel the heat of frustration building and he pulled at his shirt to loosen it over his shoulders. 'I really do have to go, Larry.'

'Nah you don't, just a couple of minutes that's all. Tell Jock who you are, tell him what happened on the weekend, your girlfriend, brothers and sisters. Say anything, just so he knows he's not alone. No-one wants to die alone, Tobe.'

'I don't know if...' Toby felt the pull of his own father a few floors away and worried about his loyalty. 'I'm a stranger.'

'Sure, you can, Jock's a good listener, he's got all day.'

The door closed and he could hear Lizard coughing and struggling in the bathroom, he thought about leaving, but knew it was wrong. He moved over to the window and sat beside Jock. The old man rolled his head to one side and looked at him. A withered right arm flexed as Jock tried to lift his hand. Toby took it, it felt white and cold, the soft papery skin folded under his touch. In that moment, he knew Jock's life had a story written in every one of those wrinkles.

'So, what have you done with your life, Mr McCutcheon?' Toby pressed his thumb and released his grip. He watched the back of Jock's hand, it went pale and the colour didn't return for some time. Toby felt the old man's life slipping from him. 'My name's Toby Farrier and it's nice to meet you Jock.' He tried to draw away, but felt Jock's hand tighten.

Wrinkled eyelids flickered open and settled shut again, he thought the old man's eyes were blue, but he couldn't be sure. Sunspots covered Jock's skin with dark splotches. A hairless scalp seemed to hang from the top of his head, like a wet tea-towel draped over dishes. He could make out the bones in Jock's arm, where withered flesh allowed purple and red skin to sag.

'Lizard says to tell you a bit about myself, but I'd rather get to know you.' Toby shot a look toward the ensuite door. 'I find it easier to listen than talk, especially when it's about me,' Toby said and imagined the old man's neck creak as Jock struggled to turn toward his voice, a faint smile creased Jock's lips. 'It seems to me you'll have a hard time talking, so I'll have a go, shall I?'

A tiny lift of an eyelid noted Jock's agreement.

Toby began talking about his early childhood and how he moved in with Pop. He thought Jock was really listening and his mood lightened. He started to tell him about his desk, and the trouble with Slasher when a nurse came in.

'Hello?' she said.

'I'm Toby.' He felt as though he'd been caught out, and his mouth went dry. 'Toby Farrier.'

'And are you family, Toby Farrier?'

He felt her tower over him. 'No, I mean, sorry, I'm not family. Lizard asked me to stay and talk to Jock for a while, he hasn't come back yet. Have you seen him?'

'He's with the physio, should be back soon.' She picked up Jock's chart and without looking up said. 'So, Toby Farrier, just how do you know Larry?'

'I don't, he wanted someone to push him back to his ward. He went to the toilet and I've been waiting for him for over an hour.' Toby wanted to go, but he felt like Jock needed him for a little longer. 'I'll give it a few more minutes and then I'd better push off.'

'Did Lizard show you Jock's album?' She opened a side table drawer, took out a photo album, and reaching across the bed passed it to Toby. 'I think the old fella would like you to see it. When he was lucid, he loved showing it to all of us, didn't you Jock?' She lifted his hand and felt for a pulse. Toby watched her eyes as she made an entry in his notes.

'He's had a full life.' She put the chart back. 'He'd make us laugh, and between coughs, tell us about some of the mischief he got up to, when he was breaking horses in the outback.' She pointed to a family photo etched into the cover. 'He'd only get sad when he talked about his wife and their children. Tears would fill his eyes and he'd say he was lucky to have been loved by them, even if it was only for the short time that they'd lived.'

Toby ran his fingers over the book's polished wooden covers. Tissue separated the black mounting pages and a silk string held it together. The tie was black with soft tassels. Toby opened it. Gilt edged, white corner mounts held black and white photos, this was a treasured item. Who were these people in the pictures, and where were they now? This was Jock's time for dying and you would think someone he was close to, would be here.

'Where are his friends? They should be here now.' Toby listened for each shallow breath.

'There's no-one.' The nurse turned away. 'He's alone, alone to die. I reckon that's why Lizard picked you. He knew Jock'll slip off soon, and he had to go out for a while. My guess is Larry didn't want him to go without anyone being here.' Her fingers combed through the few remaining strands of Jock's white hair, she wet a cloth and smoothed his eyebrows. 'You see Larry has no one either. No family or friends, sure we nurses are close to him, but Larry's lived on the street for so long, nobody cares about him. Hell, no-one even knows he's here.' She sniffed and grabbed for a tissue. 'Anyway, I'm Polly, happy to meet you Toby.'

'How long?' Toby nodded toward Jock.

'I don't know, not long now I'd reckon.' She felt for a pulse again and checked his eyes. 'Look, I know Jock would appreciate it, if you can stay until Larry gets back. It's good you're holding his hand.' Polly rubbed some cream on Jock's lips and kissed his forehead. 'I've become attached to both of them since they've been here. It's hard on all of us. We want everyone to go out with dignity. If you're religious, say a prayer for him, if not, just talk to him. Describe what you see in his photos, I know he'd like that.' She tidied Jock's bed then walked toward the nurse's station. Looking back over her shoulder she smiled and said, 'I think I like you, Toby Farrier,'

Toby looked at a picture and made up a story about it. As he talked to the old man, he'd listen to his breath halting. A couple of times he tried to drag his hand away, but Jock held on. He may have been feeble, but a little of his strength stayed with him.

Toby's eyes searched the nurse's station and the little part of the corridor he could see. There was no sign of Lizard. Desperate to see his father, he was stuck here with Jock, and began resenting it. Any other time he would be happy to stay. He shifted in the chair trying to find a more comfortable position. No, he thought, he wouldn't be. How many kids did he know, were sitting with a dying man they didn't know and telling him stories? Yes, he decided, it was official, Toby Farrier was weird. He had to be. Anybody else would just leave.

Toby stayed, telling himself another minute or two and then he'd go. A puddle of drool pooled and gathered at the corner of Jock's mouth. Toby saw it and wanted to call someone, but the nurses were gone. He swallowed hard and tried not to look, but the glob was growing and like a magnet, his eyes locked on it. Saliva started to run and followed the stubbled crack of Jock's chin. Toby gagged, he just had to do it, there was nobody else. He reached for the tissues and looking past the gloop, dabbed the old man's mouth, he gagged again. His face was close enough now to hear Jock's breath rattle up the corridor from his lungs. Jock smelled like Lizard, they both had a kind of arrowroot and mouldy bread smell. Sweet, but not in a good way, Toby was sure it was what death would smell like.

He continued his story.

Another hour passed and still Lizard had not returned. Toby felt the old man stiffen and rise; a sharp low toned moan followed. He held his own breath and waited. Jock sank into the bed and didn't breathe again. His grip loosened, and now it was Toby who held tight, he pumped at Jock's hand. Desperation and hopelessness rushed through him. He willed the old man to take another breath. He didn't, and Toby couldn't help it, he cried.

They stayed like that for a long time, Toby holding the hand of a dead man, he didn't know. With his face buried in the bedding, Toby tried to cover his anguish. It felt as if a river had burst inside him and tears ran. Years of hurt flowed onto stiff hospital sheets.

After a few minutes, he felt nurses in the room. Polly hugged him from behind. 'Come on kid, he's in a better place now. You did for him what family would do, so in that short time you were all he had, and you stayed with him to the end. Jock would have liked that.'

'I have to go now. Bloody Lizard,' Toby said. 'I could kill him.'

'No kid, I did that already.' Lizard was back. 'Ciggies, booze and drugs.'

Toby felt embarrassed and just waved him off.

'How about you sit with me too, when my time comes, I haven't got anyone who'd weep for me. I don't mean you have to cry or anything, just drop in now and then. He passed Jock's photo album to Toby. 'Here, the old bloke said I could have this, but I reckon I'd only have it a week or so and I'll be gone too.' Larry wheezed. 'Come and see me again, yeah?'

'Okay, I'm up for that.' Toby rubbed knuckles and wanted to rush out before he started blubbering again.

'Hey Tobe, this is for you too.' Lizard leaned forward and passed Toby another book.

Toby rubbed his finger along the spine and the corners felt limp, as if a dog had chewed them. 'What is it?'

'Just some scribbles Dummy. It's my sketch book. I heard you telling Jock you wanted to be a writer, so I thought I'd show you what I do. I draw stuff.' Larry held his hand out and Toby gave the book back. Larry pushed his yellow finger into the middle of the pages and opened the book to the last drawing. 'See, this is you and Jock just a while ago, you know before...'

'Yeah.' Toby swallowed and kept his eyes on the pencilled sketch, he knew if he looked at Lizard, he'd cry again.

Snapping the book shut Larry thrust it at Toby. 'It's yours.' He started to cough again and reached for his spit bottle. Toby wondered if he would ever stop trying to throw his lungs into it. After a couple of minutes Larry slumped, and appeared to dissolve into the crumple of his wheelchair. His head tilted to the left and rested on his shoulder. Light from the window caught a string of blood-lined spit; it stretched from the cup, to the lower corner of his mouth. The blood glowed like an old neon sign. Toby, repulsed at its sight, needed someone to wipe it away. He passed Lizard a tissue, Larry didn't take it.

'I can't take your book Larry.'

Lizard angled his head, and indicated for Toby to clean his mouth. He didn't want to, but he dabbed at the goo, it took more than one tissue and he kept his eyes from looking into the cup in Larry's lap. He walked hand outstretched to the waste bin, and rid himself of the tissue.

'Sure, you can, I got nothing else to give,' Lizard said.

Toby wanted to refuse, but Lizard half raised his hand stopping him.

'Please.' He coughed again, and Toby looked away. 'I got more anyway.'

'I have to go now,' Toby said.

'Yeah I know.' Lizard had a resigned sound to his voice. He reached for the call button. 'Call in again, yeah?'

'Sure.'

'Tomorrow, if I'm still here.' Larry winced, or smiled. It was hard to tell.

'Yep.' Toby felt his eyes water. 'Thanks for this.' He put the sketchpad on top of Jock's album and walked away.

CHAPTER THIRTY-NINE

The clock at the nurse's station showed three minutes to twelve when Toby reached his father's ward. He realised he had only been gone for three hours, but his time with Jock and Lizard made it seem longer. He shuddered; hospitals were starting to give him the creeps. He could hear Tracy's voice, his father might be unconscious, but no one outside the room could tell. She told him everything that happened in her world, it was as if Darren was still attentive.

'Okay if I come in?'

'Toby, Pop's worried sick. Just where have you been?' She sounded worried and relieved. 'Where have you been? Arthur said he'd give you until one o'clock and then he'd call the coppers. Jeez, Toby and to think I thought you were growing up. Here take my phone and tell Pop you're coming home now.' She shook her head. 'I don't know you at all, do I?'

'Tracy, I...'

'No, Toby I don't want to hear it. Phone Artie and go home. We'll talk about this later, I'm not having you upset me in front of Darren, just go, and take this with you.' She thrust the fountain pen at him. 'It's dangerous in his state. Take it, before I throw it out.'

'Stick your phone, I'll go home and let Pop know I'm okay, then you can all go to hell. I don't need you.' Toby had tried to keep his temper, but since he'd met Tracy again, everyone wanted a piece of him. 'I thought we were beginning to mend our rift,' he said. 'But if this is what you want, fine by me. This time though I'm not going to let you make me feel like I'm a worthless piece of crud again, Tracy. I'm better than that, and I can make it without any of you.' He felt his face redden, but he didn't care. 'I'm sick of pandering to everyone's needs. I thought you'd be better than this, Tracy, much better.' He turned and left.

Toby touched on with his Myki card, it didn't work first time, he slapped the machine and tried again, it worked. He looked up and returned the glare of the tram driver. He was sick of the grief that came from every quarter right now. If someone he didn't know peeved him, it would be enough to set him off.

He listened to the thrum of the wheels and it didn't help his mood. Mixed with the sound of the traffic and the noise of other passengers, Toby imagined he could hear the wheels saying, 'the kid's no good, the kid's no good.' It played on his mind.

Pop was at the gate waiting. He grabbed Toby's shoulder.' 'Get inside now. What's wrong with you, boy. You skived off early without a word, to God-knows-where. Sophia came around here crying, and saying you'd upset her. I had to send her home, and I took care of your sisters because you weren't here to do it. You knew I wanted to see Darren this morning, I had to let Tracy go on her own.' Spit formed blobs of cream at the corners of Pop's mouth.

Toby felt the spray of his words spattering his face. Pop's was a face red with rage, and his eyes were wide. The last time Toby had seen him like this, was the night Arthur brought him home from Kyneton. He didn't like seeing Pop so angry, but was more than ready to make his case.

'Cripes, Toby. I don't know what's got into you over the past few days. You've become a spoiled, self-centred, and obnoxious little brat. I'm going to the hospital now,

I've made the girls a couple of sandwiches, but you'll have to do dinner, and do extra for Charlie too. I told him you would.'

'But Pop, I...'

'No Toby I won't hear anything from you now.' Arthur turned away and then spun back. He grabbed Toby by both shoulders and stared into his eyes. 'You have to get a grip boy, you understand? I told Tracy you can go back and live with them when Darren comes out of hospital. She'll need someone to take care of the yard and things.' Arthur turned away.

'But Pop...'

'Talk to me after dinner, I'm off to the hospital now.'

'Pop, we need to talk.' Toby yelled at the closing door.

'Tonight.' Arthur yelled back as he opened the Magna's door. 'Now take good care of your sisters.' He shut the door, started the car and backed out of the drive in one fluid motion.

Toby wrung his hands together, grinding at the sweat in his palms. His throat felt full of sand. His tongue thick and sticking to the roof of his mouth he found it hard to breathe. His voice was gone, and he wanted to swear. Pop should understand what had happened, He felt betrayed and now his anger made him shake. How could Pop do this to him? It wasn't like him. Pop was only thinking of himself and what he'd wanted.

Toby's anger built, and old feelings stirred. Demons from his childhood were back. He never liked to remember how he'd felt, or think about what he was like back then. When he'd torn up the family home it was horrible, but now those same thoughts were back.

He didn't want to, but Toby embraced the anger and he wanted to tear this place apart too.

On the mantle, a photo showed the two of them smiling. Toby remembered Charlie had taken it at the zoo, and his mind wandered to the fun he had with these old fossils. Best of all, he remembered the three of them laughing, when one of the gorillas pooped in its hand and flung it at a yobbo in the crowd. He was eleven, and it was the first time the two of them were truly happy together. Everyone loved that picture.

Snatching it with both hands, Toby cracked it across the edge of the table. Blood started dripping from his hands where jagged glass had ripped into his fingers. Ripping it from the mangled frame he tore it in two, slid onto the floor and watched his blood pooling between his knees.

CHAPTER FORTY

Toby felt the presence of his sisters and turned; their eyes fixed on him.

Adele said, 'You had everyone worried, Tobe.'

'Yeah, you're in big trouble,' Jazz said, 'I heard Pop say so.'

'Don't take any notice of her, Toby.' Adele jumped to his defence. 'You can be a jealous little turd sometimes, can't you, Jazz? Now, say sorry to your brother for being nasty.'

'He made Pop cry, and he should be punished. I'm not saying sorry. Anyway, Adele, you're not the boss of me.'

'Hey, you two, it's okay really.' Toby stood up and rinsed his hands under the tap, 'You don't have to worry about Pop and me, we're tight.' Toby knew this wasn't finished yet, but there was no need to involve the girls. He walked to the laundry and threw the towel in with the washing. His fingers hurt from the cuts, but the gash across the heel of his thumb was deep and still bleeding.

'Adele, I'll need you to help me here. There are some steri-strips in that first aid box. I need you to get a few out and get ready to put them on, once I've cleaned the cut.' His fingers were beginning to cramp now and the pain caused his voice to quaver.

'Aw, that's gross.' Jazz said when she looked at the cuts to Toby's hand. 'I bet you're in even more trouble when Pop gets home.'

'Jazz.' Toby bent down and put his nose on hers. 'I have had as much as I can stand from you. Ever since you came here, you've been a prissy little brat, who needs a few lessons in manners. If you're here for much longer and keep it up, by God I'll teach them to you. Now go and lay on your bed until I tell you to come out.'

'I'm not doing anything you tell me.' She pouted. 'Anyway, Pop'll punish you when I tell him what you said. I'm not going to my bed. No way.'

Adele went to intervene, but Toby was too quick, and his arm held her away. 'Look, you spoiled little brat, when Pop told me to look after you he meant it. You'll go to your room, and you'll lay on your bed. If I hear a murmur out of you, I'll lock the door until your mum gets home. Do you understand?'

Toby waited, Jasmine stood there, pouted and looked at her feet. Toby lifted her chin with his good hand and made her look at him. He wanted to slap her. *Just say something and I'll make you wish you hadn't.* Satisfied she could see his rage, he whispered. 'Do you understand, Jasmine?'

'Yes...' The bravado was gone and she went to her bed. Toby heard the door slam. Her sobbing was low and long.

'She's a bitch,' Adele said.

'Nope, she's hurt and everything's strange right now. Here, help me get this fixed, I'll clean up the broken glass, then after a little while, she can come out and help with tea. Alright with you?'

'Yeah.' Adele watched Toby pour disinfectant over the cut.

He flinched.

'Hurts, does it?'

'I never get used to it,' he said. 'But I've done it heaps of times, it's either me or Pop cutting or scraping something. Always mends though. Now when I pat it dry, put the strips on one side and pull tight to the other, the blood will stop.' He smiled at her. 'How long ago did Soph go home?'

'A bit before lunch I think, she seemed upset, you know, worried. Is she your girlfriend?'

Toby jerked away so he could see Adele better and he felt his face flush. Now he couldn't even look at his sister and give her an honest answer. He didn't know if Sophia was his girlfriend, or not. He didn't know anything.

'Not sure, I've never had a girlfriend.' It was the truth. 'What do you think?' He felt the heat in his face drain away.

Adele laughed at him. 'I think she reckons she is.' She put a finger to her cheek and struck a coy pose. 'And I think you know it too. Besides she's pretty and smart, probably even smarter than you, Bro.'

'*Bro*, you watch too much television. I guess I am your *bro*.' He picked up the brush and pan, 'grab the sponge and the disinfectant for me please. I'd better get this mess and all the glass cleaned up.'

'She said she saw your zit too.'

'She saw it?' Toby raced to the bathroom and checked the mirror. He angled his face for a better look. 'Damn, I'd forgotten about it.'

'She doesn't care, said it made you more human somehow. Me, I don't know what all the fuss is about?'

'Give it a year or two and you will. Come on, do you think Jazz has had enough time in her room yet?

'Can you make it all afternoon? It's kinda nice having you all to myself again.'

'Nope, just a few minutes more okay?' Toby felt better, he was sorry for the picture, but that was a fight for another day. Pop was so besotted with his granddaughters Toby doubted he'd notice it gone.

'Come on, we can't leave her there all day, do you want to tell her?' Toby said.

'I reckon it'd be better if you did it, Bro, after all, you're the monster who her sent her there.'

'You are one smart kid Adele Farrier.' Toby put his arm around her. 'One smart kid.'

'One thing though Toby, no one tells me the truth about why you left us. I know I was just a kid, but when I ask Mum or Dad they won't say. One of the kids at my school said you had to go because you were dangerous. You don't seem dangerous to me.'

'When Dad's back on his feet, I'll talk to him about it. Until then, and as much as I'd like to tell you my side, I think it's best we let sleeping dogs lie. I don't want to stir it all up again for Pop.'

'Yeah, I get that, but if you were as bad as they say, what happened?'

'I got better okay? That's it. I had an eye problem. I don't know, it made me feel stupid and dumb, that's all it was. It's called *Convergence Insufficiency*, a condition with my eyes. Somehow, they are out of sync, and my brain was fighting to control them. I had headaches and didn't know why it was hard to read. It made me angry all the time.' Toby sighed.' Often it isn't picked up, and kids slip through the tests. Like me they get treated for ADHD and all sorts of things. Before I came to Pop, all those prescription drugs messed with my head, I was so pilled up I couldn't function. I was angry at the world and everyone in it. You can say Pop and Charlie saved me.'

Adele slipped her arms around his waist and put her head on his chest. She stayed like that for a minute or two before looking into his eyes. 'Thanks,' she said.

Toby pushed her away a little. 'C'mon let's get Jazz, she's had enough sleep now.'

'Yeah and when we do that, you'd better call Sophia, she said to call her, when you got back.'

Toby screwed his face up. He wasn't ready for another one of Soph's blasts yet.

He felt in his pocket and pulled out the fountain pen. It was sticky with sweat from Darren's hand.

'Smells like lemons,' Adele said.

'Yeah it must have dropped into Dad's cordial I reckon.'

'I hope he didn't drink it.' Adele's face shrivelled up and she shivered at the thought.

Toby said nothing. His father was comatose, but how did the lemon get on the pen. 'I'll fix it later, come on we'd better find Jazz, then I'll call Soph.'

'Call her first, trust me, Jazz can wait.'

CHAPTER FORTY-ONE

Sophia had accepted Toby's invitation to join them for dinner, and arrived just as Toby went to find Jasmine.

'We have to talk,' she said to him.

'Yeah, I know, but I have to get dinner and get everyone settled first. I'll probably have to put Pop to bed tonight too, if he's anything like he was last night.'

'Your Pop?'

'Drunk, could hardly undress himself.'

'I can't believe it, that's so cool.' Sophia giggled. 'Charlie put him to bed?'

'It's not funny, Soph, he has me running here, jumping there, and he gave me a balling out today, because he didn't know where I was. I left him a note and all. You know, I'd like Dad to get better and for everything to go back to normal, but it would be good to have a bit of peace and quiet around here again.'

'You're jealous of your sisters. That's it, isn't it?' She grinned at him, kissed her fingers and put them on his lips. 'Toby Farrier, I never thought I'd see it, but you're jealous.'

'Shh, I don't need them to know, but yeah. I guess I am a bit.'

'Let's wake your sister then.' Sophia danced backwards down the hall smiling at him, and mouthed *Toby Farrier is jealous* several times. It rankled, but he enjoyed her teasing.

Jasmine was not on her bed and Toby checked under it, he ran through the house calling her. She was there only a few minutes before. He thought of all the places he hid as a child, under Pop's bed, in the laundry cupboard. He checked them all but Jazz was gone.

'What if the mad professor has her?' he said.

'She's hiding, Jazz always hides,' Adele said, 'And she's good at it too.'

'Let me try?' Sophia said, 'you probably scare her.'

'She's frightened of Toby,' Adele said. 'And jealous too.'

'Why jealous?' Toby asked. 'No, forget that, just see if you can find her. Tell her she's not in trouble, but we need to get ready for dinner. Soph, you have to find her for me please.'

Toby headed for the kitchen, but not before he diverted through the lounge and turned the television off. Having killed the constant drone of loud kids shows, and mind numbing advertisements, he braced the sink. Potatoes needed peeling, and he had an idea to get Jazz on side, that was if they ever found her.

He listened to Sophie and Adele looking for Jasmine, and felt a huge relief when he heard Jasmine squeal. Laughter followed, and quiet words. It was good to have Sophia here. She was good with the girls.

Toby was on the last of the green vegetables when he felt a tug on the pocket of his jeans. Without turning he said. 'Hi Jazz, did you have a good sleep?'

Jasmine nodded. She still had a pouty face.

'Grab the stool from the bathroom and give me a hand with the potatoes please?'

'You mean I can help?'

'Sure, unless you want Sophia to help me?'

'No, it's okay. I'll get the stool.'

Sophia put an arm around him and gave a soft squeeze. 'Adele and I will be in the lounge until you need us, big brother.' She pulled a magazine from her bag and waved it at Adele. 'Want to see?' They moved as one and plopped onto the lounge, Toby was thankful the television stood silent.

'Sorry,' Jasmine said in such a low voice Toby strained to hear. 'Sorry I worried you and made a mess of your paper.'

Toby's heart sank. She'd touched his papers. He took a breath before speaking. 'I'm cross about the paper and you hiding, but I know what it's like to be you, too.' Toby felt the words fall, and they sounded like pasta rattling into a dry saucepan.

'Huh?' She pulled a face and stared at him.

'Look, when I was a kid I screwed up all the time and people didn't understand why. After a while, they just got tired of my tantrums. I felt ignored and it hurt. I was jealous of Adele, and I made trouble for everyone because of it.'

'Adele, you were jealous of Adele?' Jasmine screwed her nose up again.

'Yeah, she was all cute, soft and pink. I thought Mum and Dad loved her more than me. The more trouble I caused, the less they seemed to like me. In the end, I wanted to hate them because I thought they didn't love me.'

'Adele?' Jasmine shook her head. 'You thought they loved Adele more than you?'

'True, I must have been mad.'

'I think so Toby? You must have been mad alright.'

'Now, can you use a peeler?' Toby passed her the spare. 'It's the same one, Pop taught me to use. Are you ready?'

'Yep.' Jazz squared her shoulders her face tight with concentration.

Toby showed her how to start the peeler into the skin and take the peel away in long circular swirls. 'Pop can do this without breaking the peel, says it brings you luck.'

'I'll do it too.'

'Okay we'll make a competition out of it?' Toby winked, feeling her trust grow.

CHAPTER FORTY-TWO

Toby heard the back door bang and could hear Tracy, Arthur and Charlie talking as they came in.

'Smells good,' Charlie shouted. 'I guess you'll want me to carve again?' He came into the kitchen and put a consoling arm around Toby and dropping his voice said. 'Don't be too hard on Artie mate. He's frightened of losing you. He's been like a bear for the last couple of days.'

Pulling the door closed Charlie lowered his voice. 'No need for them to hear us, now what can I do to help?' He started taking plates down from the overhead cupboard.

'Pop and I have some stuff to settle, and it's not going to be pleasant either. I don't understand it, he tore me a new one today, and all for no reason.'

'I know. He came to see me just after and I told him it was strange that you didn't leave a note. He felt in his top pocket and found it. Said he put it there when he got the girls breakfast and forgot about it. Jeez, Tobe, my old mate in there couldn't love anyone more than you. He said if you left it would be a pain he doubted he'd survive. Now I know you probably think this is all just an old man's theatrics, but mate this was genuine.' Charlie's eyes were wet and he dragged the back of each hand across his cheeks. 'You have to be careful with him Tobe, and before you say it. I know you need him just as much.'

'Yeah, well it didn't seem as if I meant anything to him today. I hadn't felt that worthless for a long time. It took me back to the days before he came and got me.'

Toby wanted to grab Charlie and hug him. He needed comfort from someone, but it wasn't Charlie. He resisted and felt his soul drain, a feeling so hollow he thought all the love in the world would not make him whole again. Toby had learned to deal with the loneliness years ago, but sometimes it crushed him. He had to have it out with Pop, and soon.

'We'd better get this on the table,' he said as Sophia walked in.

'You guys okay in here?' She said slipping an arm around Toby.

Charlie asked, 'Did you do the gravy the way I showed you?'

'Always do.' He felt his spirits lift a little.

'Good lad. Elsie's recipe.' He looked at the ceiling. 'By jingo she could cook that woman. Why she married me, I'll never know?'

Tracy came in, and from behind she hugged him. 'Because, you are all warm, and cuddly, that's why.' She took the lid off a pot on the stove, sniffed it and looked at Toby. 'You did the carrots in orange juice with cinnamon?'

He nodded. 'I know Sophia and Pop like them that way.'

'Me too,' she lifted another lid, 'and you blanched the beans. Toby Farrier, you are a man of many talents.' Tracy sounded happy, but Toby sensed a melancholy about her tonight and wondered what was causing it.

Jazz took her place at the table between her mother and Sophia, she pushed the beans around on her plate. 'I don't like beans,' she said.

'You helped Toby with them, didn't you? Sophia said. 'Well you need to try these, because your brother has a magic way with beans. They are all crunchy and when you bite into them,' she closed her eyes, 'they snap with little bursts of sunshine from the fields where they grow.' Sophia turned and looking into Jasmine's eyes continued, 'if you're lucky, very lucky you might find one that tells you a story in a dream. A Toby-story, where princesses ride unicorns and honey runs down streams.'

'Really?' Jazzy's eyes widened and wanted the dream now. 'Which one?'

'That's the funny thing, you won't know until you wake up. I eat all of mine every time. I'd hate to leave one and find out next day that it was the one with the dream in it.'

'I'll give them a try.' Her fork jabbed at the green cylinder and a bean shot out. She stabbed again and lifted the bean to her mouth. 'Better than broccoli,' she said. 'But not much.'

'Any more of those beans left?' Pop said. 'I could use one of Sophia's dreams tonight.' He reached toward Jasmine's plate with his fork.

'No, these are mine,' she said and pointed to the bowl. 'You can get your own Pop.'

'So, I can little one, so I can.'

The meal finished, Toby and Sophia cleared the table while Tracy bathed the girls and got them into bed. Before they started the washing up, Toby asked her if she could help Tracy. She nodded and headed up the passage.

'Pop, can I see you for a minute?' Toby called. It was now or never. His grandfather came into the kitchen.

'You want to do this here or outside in the shed?' The old man asked.

Toby saw the fight had gone from him. Whatever his rage was this afternoon, it had gone and now he looked sad.

'I'll keep it down, Pop, I promise, but I want you to listen and not interrupt.'

Arthur nodded and sat on the stool in the corner. 'You talk, I'll listen.'

'Today you made me feel like I'm unworthy and you've never done that before. Pop, you've made me feel special from the first day I arrived here. I was a mess, but little bit by little bit, you helped me find strength. Strength to believe I mattered and over time you showed me how to behave. You taught me to respect others, you showed me how to find grace, so that I could handle their respect too. All of this you did by example and encouragement.

'I've never understood why you loved me enough to do this, but I'm beginning to. I was a nasty little kid who smashed things and beat his sister. I was rude to my parents. I didn't understand why I had to see all those doctors, why all the tests were necessary, or why I had to go away. I didn't hate anybody. I just couldn't make them understand.'

Arthur sat there saying nothing.

'And Pop, I feel a bit like that now. I don't know what I've done to make you so mad at me. I even got mad today, and broke our photo. I loved that picture.'

'I noticed; I loved that picture too.' Pop sighed.

'I wanted so much to fight with you tonight, Pop. I wanted to clear the air, but something's wrong? The fight's gone. I need you to yell at me and tell me to wake up to myself, but you're just sitting there. Are you sick?'

'Heavy of heart, that's all.'

'Pop, you really ripped into me today, and said I'd let you down. Only last night you said I should follow my instincts and make my own decisions, but you need to be consistent. I was worried about Sophia. I haven't been able to see her, and she only lives a few doors away. When I get there, she gives me a rip too. Then her mother throws me out. I didn't think it could get much worse until I saw Tracy at the hospital, and she came down on me like a ton of bricks too.'

Pop's head hung low. 'I know, Son, I know.'

Toby saw what his grandfather was going through, but needed to finish. 'Pop, you taught me never to turn anyone away, and that's what happened today. I was going to the hospital to see Dad and a bloke in a wheel chair asked me to help him to his ward. I did that, and because he needed physiotherapy, he asked me to sit with his friend in the other bed. Pop, I held old Jock's hand while he died, and all the time, all I could think about was you. I relived my life with you as I felt his life go. He slipped through my hand. He really did, it was beautiful, and painful, and wonderful, and sad, all at the same time. I wanted to share that with you because of the things you taught me. I wanted you to see I could care for someone other than myself. Cripes Pop, I need to know I'm worthy of what you've given me.'

Tears streamed from his eyes, but Toby didn't care. 'Pop all my life I've needed someone, but today, somebody I didn't know needed me and I felt worthy. It felt as if I'd learnt something and the only person who could teach me that, was you. I wanted to share it, but you just cleared off on me.'

Toby walked over and put his head on the old man's chest. Arthur's arms cradled him and he rocked as they cried.

'I was so pissed off at you, and I broke the frame in spite. I didn't think my heart could ache as much as it does, but the moment the glass broke, I broke too. Now I need you to tell me off.'

'Tobe, I wonder at times how life conspired to put us together like it has,' he said. 'One thing I can tell you though, is no-one could love you more, or be more proud. What I haven't said is how bad your Dad is.' His fingers stroked through Toby's hair. 'It doesn't look good mate. Tracy has some hard decisions to make if he doesn't improve soon.' Arthur looked up and stared at the ceiling. 'Tomorrow, you'd better go in early. We mightn't have long.'

'Charlie said you thought I wanted to go back to Kyneton?'

'Well, there's more for you there, and I thought it'd be for the best.'

Staring into eyes as puffy as his own, Toby said. 'No, Pop. My life is here in the city with you. I might want to see them at times, but I love you more than them. Pop, I need you more than them. I love Charlie and my friends too. I just know I can't live back there.'

'Pleased to hear it. Now come on, they all know we've been getting into it. Let's slip into the laundry and wash up. No one needs to know we were blubbering instead of arguing. Then I'll tell the girls a bedtime story.'

'Oh, no you don't. You and Charlie can make the dishes go away. I have fences to mend.' Toby said.

'Fair enough, we'll do them and I'll organise for takeaway tomorrow night, okay?'

Toby felt Arthur's arm, powerful, like a shield protecting him as they headed for the laundry. Right up until his grandfather reached across with the other hand, and tickled him. Things were back to normal.

CHAPTER FORTY-THREE

Toby sunk into the couch and flicked the telly on to QI. Soph nestled into his side.

Tracy cleared her throat and he looked up. She stood in the doorway. 'Hey Tobe, do you know a skinny guy from the hospital? Tattoos, heavy cough, rides a wheelchair.'

'Yeah, Lizard, why?' Toby thought about Jock dying and wanted to cry. 'He's the reason I was late getting in to see Dad. I was in palliative care with Jock.'

'Jock, who's Jock?' Charlie asked.

'Lizard, asked me to sit with him until he got back. Jock died at eleven forty-five this morning. Lizard didn't make it back in time.'

Tracy nodded. 'The guy in the wheelchair, you said he's called Lizard?'

'He found me with Darren. Came up to tell me that you're a good kid and I wondered why he'd say it?' Tracy pursed her lips and swallowed. 'It was because of Jock, wasn't it?'

Toby gave a half-formed smile. It was such a strange time, but he was glad he'd been there for Jock.

'He found me again as I came out of the lift and asked me to give you this.' She held up a ring. 'I've given it a bit of a clean, but a jeweller would really make it sparkle. Might only be glass, but it's a nice memento considering the circumstances.'

Tracy slipped it onto her index finger and showed her hand to Sophia.

'Has to be a man's ring,' Sophia said. 'It's too big and too masculine for a woman.'

Tracy slid it off her finger and dropped it into Toby's hand. It felt like catching a river stone, smooth and heavy. Toby saw the age in it and held it to the light. The clarity of the red stone was beautiful, no grind marks or inclusions. He studied it for a minute and passing it to Arthur, stood up and kissed Tracy.

'Thanks.' The ring reminded him of the one that Shamus had written about. Would it be too crazy to think it was the same ring? He pulled Sophia out of the chair. 'Come with me.' He held her hand and sped off to his room.

Toby and Sophia were looking at the notebook when there was a knock on his door.

'Can I come in?' Tracy said.

Sophia looked at Toby. He nodded and put the book on the bed.

'Sure, just a sec,' She said.

They dragged the boxes away from the door.

'Come in.' Sophia opened the door. 'It took ages, but we found it.'

Tracy stepped in tentatively. 'Found what?' Tracy frowned.

'Here look,' Toby said. 'This ring was always on Banker Bill Ryan's right hand.' He showed the cutting to his stepmother. 'If it is the same ring and the mad professor is related to Banker Bill, this could hold the key to everything.'

'Might be more than one ring though,' Tracy whispered.

'I'm checking the gold marks register now,' Sophia said. She had the computer open and was looking at the list on the screen.

'We found the picture, and then we started to flatten out the screwed-up paper. I know I should just toss it in the bin,' Toby said to her, 'but it's really old, and for reasons I can't explain, I need to keep it.'

'I have to iron the kid's clothes sometime tomorrow. If it can wait until then, I'll show you how I saved my homework after I'd tossed a wobbly and screwed it up,' Tracy said. 'Look I've still got some work to do, so I'll see you tomorrow.'

'And when Toby's not around you can tell me about the boys you went to school with,' Sophia said. 'You know, woman to woman.'

Tracy laughed. 'Girl to girl is more fun.'

Toby stared at O'Tooles notes.

'Tobe,' Tracy's words came soft and had a shakiness to them. 'Tonight when I was talking to your friend Lizard, he told me I should be proud of you.' She paused. 'And I am, but then he said I'd done a good job raising you. I was too ashamed to tell him I didn't, that it was Arthur who brought you up.' She put her hand over her face and walked out of the room shaking her head and sniffing.

Toby wanted to chase after her, but Sophia held him back. 'Let her go,' she said.

He could hear Tracy sobbing. He stood up.

Sophia grabbed his hand. 'Leave her, she needs this now. Trust me, Toby I know about this stuff.'

'Because you're a girl?'

'Because, I'm a woman.' She pushed him back on the bed and jumped on him, pinning him down. She pushed her hair away from his face and started exploring his lips with hers.

They had kissed the other night, but this was better. She pulled away, rolled onto her side and faced him. His arm was under her neck and he rubbed her shoulder with his hand. He was smiling at her.

'We'll have to practise that again,' Sophia said.

'Keep going until we get it right you mean?' He began tracing her shoulder blade with his finger.

'Something like that.' She sat up and straightened her top. Her legs swung over the side of the bed. Rubbing his knee, she felt him sitting alongside her. Toby put his arm over her shoulder. She lifted it away. Toby kissed her again, it was gentle but he felt he shouldn't linger, more of a peck this time. Sophia had made him feel wonderful, making him whole again. 'How does that happen?' he said.

'Well I just jumped you and...'

'No, not that, I mean today and this. Everything. I was spoiling for a row with Pop. From the time I got up this morning everyone made me feel like dirt. The only good thing I did was to hold the hand of a man when he died. It made me so sad. Then Jasmine going missing and all...I just wanted to curl up and howl.' He slipped off the bed and faced her; he was on his knees and he felt her legs across his hips. Her ankles crossed and he leant back so he could see her properly. 'And now you kiss me like that, and everything melts into space. I don't know how you do it. Maybe it's hormones, maybe it's not. I just know I want to be with you.' He leaned in and kissed her lips again. 'Now I'd better walk you home before your mum comes looking for us.'

Laughing at him she said, 'we can wait a little bit longer,' and kissed him again.

CHAPTER FORTY-FOUR

Leaving Sophia at her door, Toby waved at the police patrol as they cruised past before he slipped back into the house. Someone was in the shower, probably Tracy, and everyone else was asleep. It was nice to have some quiet. He wandered into the kitchen and opened the fridge. Milk. That's what he needed. He pulled a glass out and filled it up.

'Hey Toby.' He wheeled around.

'Tracy. I was just getting a drink. You?' He raised his glass.

'I'm fine thanks, I just wondered if you looked at any of your Dad's old log books yet?'

'Sorry, I seem to be collecting old books at the moment. One of them feels haunted, as if it has a hold over me. I have to solve this puzzle. The log books,' he looked at his feet. 'It's all a bit raw, sorry.'

'Yeah, I understand, but do you know why I gave them to you?' She pulled a chair out from the table and pointed for him to sit down.

'Not really, I thought they were like a personal effect. Even though I haven't read them, they help me feel closer to him.'

'That's good.' Tracy moved behind him and drew out a chair for herself. She moved back and bent down putting her arms around him. He could smell her freshness from the shower. He thought it was nice, and her touch was gentle, much like he imagined a mother's would.

'What you don't know then, is that every day after you left, your dad ached for you.' She squeezed and her touch was warm. 'I wasn't much help, and he dealt with the guilt of estranging you the only way he could. He wrote his feelings down. A truckie always has paper and a pen, so whenever he filled out his logbook, he wrote a letter to you on the back of the page. He thought he'd kept it hidden from me, and for a long time he did.' Toby felt her head on his. 'One day I noticed he was folding the pages back under. As I told you, most drivers fold the paper in on itself covering the day's log. Well from the day you left, your dad did it differently, he could hide his letters that way.'

'So, he missed me too?'

'Every minute I'd say. He'd cut us off because he couldn't bear to be without you.' She sat down and dragged Toby's glass toward her. 'Every so often we'd get some news from John through Terri, or another local who'd known Arthur. We saw how well you were doing.' Tracy let go of his shoulder and sat down in the chair next to him. 'We totally failed you, Tobe...'

Silence started to crush him. Toby sucked in a few deep breaths and let them expire, long and slow.

'I'm not sure that's right.' He heard the words, but it was as if somebody else had spoken them, it didn't sound like him. 'I was a handful and Pop took me on, kinda like a project. A bit like that book, Papillion. He moulded and shaped me to a point where I valued myself. Back then, I didn't like myself much, and I didn't help you to like me either.' He felt her hand on his. 'But I reckon I've come to the point where you can all like me. Our next step is to build it to where you can love me.'

'I'm not sure that I don't already.' She rubbed his hand without looking up. 'I'd say we have both loved you since the day you were born.'

She pulled a yellowing Polaroid picture from the pocket of her dressing gown and put it in front of them on the table. 'This is us. Terri, John Evan's sister, Michelle—your mum—and me. We're at home in the front room and that bundle on your mum's lap, is you. There's enough love in this photo to power a nuclear submarine.'

Toby waited for her to say something more, but she didn't.

'I...' He too found it hard to speak. The clock ticked above the noise of the distant traffic. It sounded louder with each tick and he was convinced it would deafen them. 'Trace, I need all of you. Pop and me were lonely knowing you were out of reach.'

She hugged him again. 'I know, and that's why I'm talking to you now.' She stood up. Her arms were wide, 'Come here, mate.'

He leant against her and she enfolded him.

'I think they are going to ask me to turn off your dad's life support. It might be tomorrow. It might be in a couple of days.' She was sobbing now.

Toby could feel her shaking under her robe. He felt his tears run too.

'I want you to spend the day with him tomorrow. I want you to tell him stories. I want him to feel you on his skin. Toby, I want you to know him. I don't know. I just hope he's in there trying to get out, and I reckon if he doesn't respond for you, then maybe...' She turned her face away, caught her breath and said, 'Maybe he's gone already.'

Toby nodded and they stood there, mother and son, embraced as one.

CHAPTER FORTY-FIVE

Toby lay on his bed staring at the ceiling, his eyes accustomed to the dark. Red and blue pilot lights on the various chargers mingled with the amber readout of the clock. He could see everything. The house was alive with sleeping sounds. He could hear Pop's slow and heavy breathing, rattling in and out. It was a familiar noise, secure and comforting. Jazz had to be on her back in the next room, because he could hear her too. Her snoring was softer and shallow. Adele was dreaming and talking in her sleep. He smiled at her laughing, and he thought she must have been dreaming about someone tickling her. She giggled again and he wanted to laugh too.

It was different for Tracy and he thought she was having a night like his. At first, he heard her crying and then it stopped. He knew she wasn't asleep because he could hear her rolling over in bed. He heard the thumping of her fist as she pounded the pillows into shape and the crying would start again. She walked to the kitchen. The tap ran and he could hear the sound change as she tested the temperature with her finger. He heard the glass fill and the squeak the cold tap made as it turned off. Tonight, he had a different view of his stepmother, and he started to understand his childhood better. The passage board outside his door creaked, you didn't notice it during the day, but now it sounded like a siren.

Tracy tapped on his door. 'You still awake, mate?' She waited, then turned the door knob. 'Can I come in?'

'Yeah, I can't sleep either.'

'I have so much going on in my mind right now, I don't seem to know if I'm coming or going.' She rubbed her hands over her arms. 'I'm going into the hospital, I haven't slept with Darren since the accident, and tonight I need him more than you could imagine. Will you tell Arthur where I am, and help with your sisters until I come home? I just need him tonight Tobe, do you understand?' She moved to sit on the bed.

He moved his legs away. 'I understand, and I feel it too.'

'Is your phone charged?' she said.

'It is now; I put it on charge when I got home.'

'Good, tell me the number.' She entered it into her contacts. 'I'll send you a selfie of your Dad and me okay?'

'I'd like that.' He rolled onto his side and looked at the pile of crumpled paper on top of the filing cabinet.

'I think Jazz and me are gunna make it,' he said. 'She helped with the veggies tonight.'

'She can be a bit hard to handle at times. I say it comes from the Farrier side. Darren says different though. Now, I'd better toss on some trackies and get into the hospital.'

She stood up. 'And Sophia, I think she's lovely, a good fit for you.' His phone blinked with a message; Tracy passed it to him. 'Speak of the devil,' she said, and left him to Sophia's text.

Toby heard Tracy back out of the driveway as he was replying to Sophia's tenth text. She wanted to know everything that happened between him and his stepmother. It felt like gossip, but Toby indulged her.

CHAPTER FORTY-SIX

Feeling like he hadn't slept at all, Toby saw the dawn streaming in through his window. He had meant to draw the blind last night, but he also liked seeing the shadows that the tree outside his room cast over everything. He felt someone jump on his bed and crawl under the sheet.

'Know what I want for breakfast?' Jasmine said as she snuggled in to him.

He felt her body all soft and warm. So, this is what it's like to have a kid sister. He smiled at her and brushed the hair away from her eyes. 'I have no idea, fried porcupine brains with dinosaur eggs?'

'Nope, pancakes.' She pushed her elbows in and dragged her knees up making a ball.

'Pop made you pancakes yesterday.'

'But he said you do it better.'

'I'll bet he did. Let me get showered and dressed and then pancakes it is.' He tickled her. 'Now get out of here, dress yourself and brush that hair.'

She wriggled out and dropped onto the floor. 'Sorry about the mess I made yesterday.'

'I was cross, but I'm fine with it now. You were angry and hurt, that's all,' he said. 'Now tell your sister to get dressed, and make your beds too.'

He pulled Larry's sketch book out and flicked through the pages. Some of them were dark with demons and cobwebs, others were of the city. Old buildings were a favourite. People too, street people, old women pushing laden shopping carts. One scene was under the Queen Street Bridge, the people in the camp were rough and dirty. Shanties made of cardboard boxes with torn up paper and rags for bedding. It wasn't much of a way to live.

'You haven't even had your shower yet.' Jazz stood in the door way, her hands on her hips, wearing a frown cold enough to freeze fire. 'Adele's getting dressed. Hurry up.'

Toby closed the book, and pulled up his bed. 'I'm going now, okay?'

'I'm hungry.'

'And I'm on it. Turn the telly on if you like.' He grabbed a pair of shorts and his underwear and headed to the shower.

Toby took the ring out of his pocket and was looking at it when Tracy came home. She said there was no change in his dad's condition and it was okay if he wanted to spend the day at the hospital. However, he should know that they had put Darren back onto the ventilator and when she left him this morning, it was still controlling his breathing. Toby wondered how much more he could handle. Getting to know his sisters and Tracy, was one thing, but talking to his dad, saying sorry and telling him how much he loved him, was all he wanted to do. To hear his dad's voice again, would be something else. He felt goose bumps on his skin and rubbed the ring along his arm. The cold of the stone tickled and a cold shiver went through him.

Tracy and the girls were taking Pop to Kyneton today. They would show him their horses while Tracy planned the work and rostered staff for the coming week. The day was his. Toby planned to see Sophia on his way to the hospital and she would meet him there later. The police had told her family they thought the attack was a one off, but would continue to send a patrol car past the house a few times at night. Daytime patrols would cease as they considered the danger had passed.

CHAPTER FORTY-SEVEN

Toby rubbed the back of his father's hand. It felt warm, which he considered a good sign. He watched the monitors and found himself mesmerised by trace lines on the screen. The beeps from other equipment in the ward would sometimes coincide and for a while they stayed in time. To Toby the noise was a comfort, while there was movement and noise there was hope.

Reading one of the letters in his dad's log book made his insides churn, so instead, Toby unfolded each page to read the trip lines. He asked his dad questions about where he went, and what happened. Before long Toby began to work a story into the logs. He knew the names of Darren's dogs, because there was a note to say which one had worked that day. By midday Toby had a complete story line in his head and making notes in a pocket book so he could recreate it on his computer when he was home.

A young nurse with a headscarf came in. She felt his dad's pulse and made notes on his dad's chart. Toby watched for any change in her expression. Nothing.

She put the chart in the rack and touched his shoulder. 'Get some lunch. I have to check his drains and change a couple of dressings. He'll be okay with me. I've prayed to Allah that he survives.'

Toby thought her smile genuine and had warmth about it he couldn't explain.

'Maybe a prayer to his god will help too.'

'His god?' Toby said. 'I thought he didn't believe.'

'Maybe he doesn't, maybe you don't either.' She checked his notes and smiled again. 'He has Presbyterian written on his chart, so it was important to someone that we record it.' She looked into Toby's eyes. 'Sometimes it doesn't hurt for one to believe in a superior being. I know my faith has helped me overcome difficult times.' She looked up as she pulled the curtain around the bed. 'What have you to lose? Your prayer could be the only thing needed now. If it is, don't you think it would be a shame not to ask his god for help?' She squeezed Toby's forearm. 'Now run off, I'll be about twenty minutes, and when you come back he'll be all fresh and clean.'

Toby dragged a tatty old teddy bear from his pack. 'This was Pop's, then Dad had it, and I kept it when I left home.' He brushed the fur and tried to suppress his embarrassment of having the toy. 'He's a bit scruffy, but will you put it in Dad's hand when you are finished.'

'What's this bear's name?' She said.

'We all called him, Ted, just Ted.'

She held the bear out and then cradled him like a newborn baby. 'Well, Ted, I'm Miriam and I think you might be just the trick needed here today.'

She put him on the side table. Her movements were soft and tender. Toby could see she cared. One who possesses grace, he thought.

'My shift finishes at two,' she said. 'Ted, I'll come back and say goodbye to you before I go.' She winked at Toby. 'Now shoo.'

He walked out and looked over his shoulder, the curtain was drawn and he could hear Miriam talking to his father explaining each little procedure.

It comforted him knowing Miriam was with his dad.

CHAPTER FORTY-EIGHT

Toby woke to a nurse—different to Miriam—shaking him; he had fallen asleep on his father's pillow.

'Toby, wake up. I have palliative care on the phone. They say Larry O'Toole has asked for you. Can I tell them you are coming?' Her voice was sharp.

He shook his head and rubbed his eyes with the back of his hands. He wanted to yawn, but suppressed it. He looked at the clock on the monitor. A bit after three, Pop and the girls should be coming home soon. Stretching he checked the monitors, everything was the same as when he fell to sleep.

'Toby?' she said. Her stare drilled holes through him. 'What do I tell them?'

'I'm on my way now.' He grabbed his backpack and swung one strap over his shoulder.

'I'll be back when I can, Dad. Don't go anywhere.'

He blew a kiss and ran to the lifts. He'd only met Lizard yesterday, but he promised him this. Not because of the ring, but for the trust. *Why does everything happen to me?* He didn't ask to be the one whose job it was to hold the hands of the dying. *Toby Farrier has a life to lead. I'll do this for Lizard, but from then on, it's all about me.*

His mind drifted, the doors opened. The lift was crowded and behind a group of people he saw Slasher and his mum. Toby looked down, hoping they didn't see him, hit the button for Larry's floor and shrunk back into the corner of the lift. He couldn't take another blast from Slash today. Toby had to sort something out with him soon. It was hard work carrying this grudge around, and he knew Danny must feel it too.

Palliative care was serene compared to other places in the hospital, not exactly quiet, but everyone spoke in soft tones. The televisions that were working were mute, and he couldn't hear any mobile phones begging to be answered. He told the nurse's station who he was and an older woman showed him to where Larry slept.

'He asked me to pack his things. They are in a shopping bag in his cabinet. He said not to give them to you until he's gone,' she said.

'Where should I sit?'

'Anywhere you're comfortable. Yesterday the girls said you were here with Jock. I think, what you did for him, Larry would like too. He can't talk anymore; his breath is slow. Pneumonia has been taking him a little more each day. He asked me to write you a letter last night. I put it in the bag with his things. You have to promise not to open it before you get home though. He insisted I got you to agree to that.'

'I don't understand, but why?'

'You will when you read it.' She moved over and put an arm around him. It seemed everyone was hugging him lately. 'Now I'll bring you a cup of tea and a biscuit or two, okay?'

'Thanks,' was all he could say.

Toby reached for Larry's hand and held it. It felt the same as Jock's had. He remembered what the nurse said about faith this morning. If anyone could use a prayer right now, it was Lizard.

Toby closed his eyes, searching for something to say to God about a man he didn't know. He knew the Lord's Prayer; he would start with that and work his way up. After the prayer, Toby told Lizard about the desk, and its secrets. Not the least of which was the fountain pen. He talked about the way it smelled of lemon. He spoke of his father's accident, and the changes it caused to the family.

There were no wires and no monitor to beep when a drip line emptied. Larry the Lizard was serene. The ink in his tattoos appeared brighter and his skin had lost the last of its yellow. The ever-moving tongue from yesterday now hung from the corner of his mouth, and every few minutes, Toby would dab drool with a tissue. He refused the offer of gloves from one of the nurses. It didn't feel real to him, and he was sure it wasn't something Larry would want.

Toby wanted to say something. He'd seen priests deliver the last rights in movies, and could almost remember the words, but he would feel a fake if he said them. A prayer for Larry needed to be something more original. He lifted Larry's hand and clasped it between his.

Using his legs, he dragged the chair closer, rested his elbows on the bed and thought about what he needed to say. Sure, he could say the words in his mind, but that wouldn't be a real prayer. No, he would say them aloud, and if others could hear, then maybe Larry's god would too.

'Dear Heavenly Father.' No, that sounds too corporate and, Larry was by no means that.

Toby shut his eyes and started again. 'God, if you can hear me, I'm praying for my friend Larry, I don't know much about him, Lord, but I'm sure you'll have a record of his life up there somewhere. Well, I'm asking you to overlook any of the bad stuff Larry might have done, and to tote up his list of good stuff, please. I only met him yesterday and yet he showed me how to offer compassion to a stranger, something I never fully understood before. When he asked me to hold Jock's hand yesterday, I didn't think I could do it. Right there, he taught me how to value the knowledge of a life well lived. Larry gave me that opportunity and I'm stronger because of it.

'Even when his lungs were filling with fluid, he would con someone to take him out for a smoke, seeing the way he did that, I now understand the power of persuasive negotiation. Larry showed me, that by taking a cigarette to his lips in his last days, that no matter how weak you feel, you can stand against popular opinion. I'm not saying I wish to smoke, I don't, but that Larry cared about people, not their opinion of him. He knew exactly who he was and his body art defined him. He was proud of who he was.

'Most of all, Lord, I understand from teachings and what I've read, that you're a caring and forgiving God. In one day, Larry taught me why we should put others first. He has shown me that you go out of life with nothing. I learned that when he gave his ring to me. You see, Lord, he couldn't be sure I'd come back, but he wanted me to have it anyway. So, he showed me the value of faith. By asking me to sit here with him, Lord he's taught me the value of trust and through this prayer, humility.

'Lord, Larry's had enough trouble in his life. I've seen it in his drawings, they show enough pain and conflict to fill the M.C.G. I don't know if he has any family. Even if he does, he chose me for this, and I am humble.

'Lord, I'm asking you to take this ragged, painted angel, my friend Lizard into your arms and treasure him as a gift. When you receive his soul, thank him for me. I will never forget him.'

Toby paused and while he waited, his eyes moistened and he wanted to wipe them, but resisted, he still held Larry's hand.

'Amen.'

Toby stayed there with his eyes closed for what felt like ten minutes, still holding Larry's hand. The room felt so serene, he felt a hand on his shoulder, and heard his name.

'Toby, it is okay to let his hand go now,' the nurse said. She rubbed his neck. 'Larry's gone.' Her voice was mature and melodic, but he didn't want to hear it. When he looked at her, she smiled; he'd seen her at the nurse's station yesterday.

'No, he can't be, I can feel his hand, it's still warm.'

'He slipped away about halfway through your prayer. I didn't want to stop you. It's funny, Larry kinda smiled and that was it, his pulse stopped.'

'How did you know?'

'I came in when I heard you, and wanted to hear what you were saying. I felt for his pulse the whole time. We both held him while he died and I think he'd have liked that.'

'Really, he went then?' Toby didn't know what to feel, or how to react.

'Come now, we'll leave him in peace. The others will be in to get him soon, and you don't need to be here for that.'

She put an arm around him. 'Have you known Larry long?'

'Since yesterday, that's all.' As he said it, he felt lighter and the sense was amazing. He choked on his words. 'But, yeah, we were mates.'

'Here, you'd better take your stuff. Larry said to ditch anything you didn't want. Old Jock and Larry had new wills drawn up only last week leaving their stuff to each other. They thought it was a bit of a lark and joked about who would go first. They made a pact to be with each other at the end, and part of that pact was to go out with dignity. You helped them do that. Last night Larry organised a new will. I don't know why, because I don't think either of them had anything, but the paperwork is all legal and is all in here.'

She handed him two envelopes.

'No, don't open it now. Wait until you get home.'

'Home, I've got to see Dad, everyone will wonder where I am.'

She handed him two shopping bags. 'Not a lot to show for two lifetimes, is it?' She shrugged at the thought of leaving such a small trace of their existence. 'Their clothes went to the incinerator weeks ago, it's only mementoes in here.' She tapped the bags. 'I'll ask an orderly to help.'

Sophia sat in the chair beside Darren and stroked his arm. She looked up and said hello when he came back in. Toby put Lizard's bags behind her chair and checked the monitors. He tried to recall their readings before he left, they were much as before. Ted snuggled in under Darren's left forearm, he looked satisfied even if one eye did hang by a cord.

He bent down and kissed Sophia's lips. She lifted her hand to his hair and held him there. It felt good and he wanted more.

Someone came in the room.

'Wow! Power kissing, now I remember being young and doing that.' Nurse Robert held his hand to his mouth and winked.

'Sorry, I didn't hear you' Toby said, his mind raced for something clever to say to cover the embarrassment he felt was written red on his face.

Sophia just laughed. 'I think he's getting the hang of it now,' she said.

'I have to turn Darren again now, check his wounds and things. You can leave him to me. I'd suggest the coffee shop and a bit more practice on your tonsil tennis.'

He patted Toby's back. 'I'll take good care of your dad, okay?'

'I know you will. Ta.' Toby checked the time. 'We'd better head home anyway. My stepmother should be here later.' He looked at the machines. 'Which one shows his brain activity?'

'We aren't monitoring that.' Robert said.

'Why not?'

'The doctor will explain it to his wife, if she asks. It just isn't normal practice, in a case like this.'

'Do it for me, yeah?' Toby said. 'Look if it's a signature that's needed get me a form and I'll sign it. Hell, it's only a piece of equipment.'

'Why do you want us to do that?'

'Just imagine if it was you lying there, unable to communicate. People prodding and poking at you. Talking about you and saying things that affect your life. You can hear everything they're saying, you want to scream and tell everyone that you're still in there; you are alive and trapped, unable to get out.' Toby turned to face the nurse. 'Imagine yourself buried in setting concrete, only your head out and no one can hear you. How frustrating would that be, Robert? You'll die, and there's nothing you can do about it.

'No one's going to flick those switches and let him die without knowing if his brain is active.' Toby looked into the nurse's eyes. 'Do you understand what I'm saying?'

'I don't know how, but by the time your step mother gets here, I'll have a monitor for him. My promise to you.'

Toby put out his hand, 'we have a deal then.'

Robert shook it, 'we do.'

Sophia picked up one of the green bags and Toby took the other. She had her own bag over the same shoulder. Toby took her hand and it felt wonderful.

The tram rattled and swayed its way along Royal Parade and with every movement their bodies rubbed closer. Soph's hand felt warm and tiny compared to the men whose hands he'd held in the past two days.

Sophia shivered.

'Are you okay?'

'Yeah, someone just walked over my grave that's all.'

Toby thought it was a silly phrase and he had never understood why people used it. Maybe it was a tool to understand the unexplainable.

'Good.' He said and squeezed her.

He withdrew his arm and took out the letter from Larry. A key dropped onto the floor of the tram. Sophia picked it up and studied it while Toby read the letter.

Toby couldn't stop the tears as he read. He dug around in his pocket for a handkerchief. He passed the letter to Sophia. 'I thought he was homeless, at least, he looked homeless. Read this.'

Sophia passed him the key and read the letter.

The key was heavy, like one of those used on a heavy padlock. He turned it over in his hand. A key to a mystery.

She looked up and started laughing. 'A key to a squat?' the idea tickled her, 'your new friend Lizard left you his squat, that's just classic.'

Toby opened the other envelope. The letter was from a legal office. Larry did have some wealth and a property. His solicitor held the deed and other papers in trust. Attached to it was an invitation to schedule an appointment. Toby had immediate access to the property, but he couldn't change anything. Larry had placed a covenant on it. He wanted to scream with joy, but conflicting emotions rippled through him.

Toby reached for Sophia's hand. 'I'm glad you came.' He leaned in to kiss her. The moving tram rocked their embrace. It was such a nice feeling they nearly missed their stop. 'I don't want this to end,' he said.

'Me neither,' Sophia said, picking up the bags. 'But we've have to get off here.'

For two blocks, they walked without saying a word. Holding hands was enough.

CHAPTER FORTY-NINE

The noise from the Farrier house was chaotic. The curtains were open and they could see Charlie showing the girls his piano accordion, and how it worked. Toby winked at Sophia and kissed her cheek. He shrugged his backpack, making it more comfortable and so he could hold her. He leant back against the fence post, pulled her to him and kissed her.

A runner jogged past interrupting them. They pulled apart and Sophia lifted her hand to wave at him. The jogger disappeared through the park and she pushed away from Toby.

'Look I've got to run. Pizza at your place, yeah?

'Who was that?' Toby said.

'I don't know? Just some jogger.' She kissed his cheek.

Holding her hand tightly. He didn't want this moment with her to finish.

She dragged it away. 'I'll be back soon.' She grinned, then turned and skipped back down the street to her house.

Pushing the door open, Toby's mind was on the jogger and it nagged at him. It wasn't something that happened on this street at this time of night. The regulars were either early morning or those who ran after the morning school drop off.

'Be with you in a minute,' he called to Pop who he heard in the kitchen.

'All under control, Tobe.'

His head full of chaotic thoughts he put the bags in his room, washed his hands and headed back to his grandfather.

'Charlie's giving the squeezebox a good work out tonight, Pop.'

'A new audience, how were things?'

'I don't know. I'm not sure how to feel, Larry died today and left me everything, well when I say everything, I mean his squat and some stuff in those bags, and while I'm sad that he died, I'm excited to see this squat if it really exists. Dad's hooked up to machines they say are keeping him alive and yet there's no monitor to see if his brain is working, and I'm angry about that. I think I'm falling in love and I don't know if that's putting Sophia in danger.'

'Whoa, that's way too much to take in all at once. Better we break it down into little chunks and work through it that way.' Arthur stretched an arm around his grandson. 'We'll get this lot fed and we will get a handle on it, okay?'

'Okay. Anyway, what's with all the noise?'

'If Tracy has to give the okay for them to switch the machines off tomorrow, I thought we could all use a bit of frivolity tonight. Take our minds off the inevitable sorrow we'll feel later.'

'Where's Tracy now?'

Arthur looked at the kitchen clock, 'with Darren I'd reckon. She wants to spend as much time with him as she can. We all do.'

'Do you reckon the bloke who attacked Sophia has been picked up yet?'

'The cop cars keep going past on the hour, so I'd say not yet. Why?'

'A bloke jogged past as we stopped at the gate and it gave me the shivers. I just want them to lock up that bloody professor and throw away the key.'

'Look if he's out there they'll get him; besides we don't know it was him who attacked Soph.'

'No, but it was him who hurt me.'

More people were arriving now and Charlie's feet were stomping the beat as he pumped out sixties rock and roll on the piano accordion. From the window, Toby saw the police constables parking John's car as Tracy's four-wheel drive squealed into the drive.

Once inside, Tracy called the family together and ushered them into Arthur's room. She told them the doctors had changed their minds. There would be no switching off Darren's life support systems and he was going to another ward. The nurse Toby had spoken to had organised a new monitor and it showed Darren had brain function. He was responding to simple questions, but they warned caution, telling her not to get her hopes up and not to broadcast it yet. Toby saw his grandfather's sadness lift, tonight they would have reasons to celebrate, a night of hope and togetherness in the company of friends.

Before the pizza arrived, Arthur stood to welcome everyone thanked them for coming and apologised for not providing beer or spirits, but Tuesdays are not drinking nights by his reckoning.

Toby squeezed Sophia's hand, 'he can go on a bit when he gets like this,' he said, 'you watch. In a minute tears'll flood and he'll be blubbering. This is embarrassing.'

'He'll say something about you next.' Sophia said.

'I don't think so. Since the girls came to stay, he hasn't even seen me. I didn't exist for the first couple of days.'

'Shh.' Sophia said. 'I want to listen. Here we go.'

Arthur held up a photo, it was the same as the one Toby smashed. 'A few days ago, pressure from outside the family broke our little gang apart and I failed to see it. Charlie knew, Toby knew, but I got so caught up in myself, and what I wanted. I forgot what was important. Toby, I treated you badly and in front of our friends I want to say sorry.'

'It's not necessary, Pop, you know that.' Toby called from the end of the table.

'Well I think it is, and as I have always said, my house, my rules.'

'Thanks, Pop,' Toby said. 'Now I reckon Charlie must have a story to tell.

Arthur thanked everyone again, toasted Darren, Tracy and the girls, and sat down.

CHAPTER FIFTY

Charlie had the floor, and from the look of it, he was in his element. He cleared his throat and waited for everyone to quiet down. 'I saw an old friend today and showed him pictures of Toby's ring. Saul knew the ring and some of the history behind it. Do you want to hear?' Charlie pumped the accordion to highlight the question. Everyone clapped. He pushed back from the table and looked everyone in the eye. He opened the accordion, its sound mournful, set the story as a drama.

Charlie was ready, the crowd hushed and with a squeeze, his story started.

'Banker Bill Ryan was not such a mean man, more of a calculating one. He'd watched on as his father and uncles failed at the diggings. As much as they followed each rush for gold, by the end of the nineteenth century, the family were still penniless.'

William Wyatt stood up and signalled to Charlie to halt his story for a moment. Slasher's mum was standing next to him. 'Thanks for the hospitality everyone, but we have another engagement. So, if you'll excuse us, we'll say goodnight.'

Toby watched as they left and wondered what Slasher thought of his mum fooling around with old Mr Wyatt. That'll make interesting times in the school yard next term.

Charlie continued once the door slammed shut. 'On the diggings twelve-year-old Bill witnessed firsthand the futility in shifting dirt for little reward. He decided he wanted something more. A rudimentary education in a shanty school house had taught him how to count, read and write. Good tools for someone in the city, but wasted as a digger.'

The accordion squawked once more and someone clapped.

'A young William Ryan however, found a way to build his fortune on the diggings. Men paid him to run errands and by the time he was fourteen, he had enough money to set up his own store. He catered for the whims of the diggers and their wives.

'Smart enough to understand compound interest, a lesson learned when he defaulted on an account in Mr Myer's store. Young Bill Ryan saw the benefit of selling goods on credit, and on credit, he was vigilant. Each day he would total his ledgers. If the client's account was outstanding, Bill would add a percentage, a late payment fee he called it. No more than a boy, Bill Ryan soon had financial control of many men.'

Charlie rubbed his hands together, scrooge like. 'One night a digger Pickaxe Jack, unhappy with the way his account had blown out over the month and spiteful about the way Bill had accosted his wife for payment, showed up at Bill's door. He gave our young entrepreneur a hell of a beating. That little altercation prompted Bill to change his plans.'

Arthur interrupted and asked if everyone had enough to eat.

Another squeeze grabbed their attention and Charlie continued the story. 'Jack was a rough, hard drinking digger, who owed Bill plenty, and with no hope of settling his account, Bill offered Jack a job. When a debt was overdue, Jack was there, he took part of his fee in cash and the balance reduced his account.

'Bill had enough of the squalor, and of dirty men with uncouth habits. He knew the gold would run out and thought it wise to leave before it did. On news of the next big strike, he'd sell. He didn't have to wait long. Patrick Long hauled out a twenty-ounce nugget and the camp went wild. Bill Ryan sold the business to one of the late arriving diggers and broke camp. He had a tidy profit. It was time to build a bank and he made sure Pickaxe Jack went too.'

Charlie accented his story with another squeeze of the accordion. 'Bill was ready, moving to Melbourne and leasing a shopfront on Collins Street, he opened the Investment Bank of Ireland and Victoria. He'd studied much about the benefits of interest and he loved the foreclosure laws of the time. Jack had sobered up and bought a nice property on the Maribyrnong River. Debt collection served him well, and his small farm became a model for horse breeders of the area.'

He stopped talking abruptly at the sound of a cat cry followed by a large thump. Toby looked out to the darkness, but saw nothing. Charlie looked out as well. Someone—was it Nathan's mum?—said they wanted to go inside, and everyone followed. Toby lingered while Ben and Nathan took a leak down by the back fence. He hoped they would be able to come with him and Soph tomorrow to see the squat Lizard had left him.

CHAPTER FIFTY-ONE

With their visitors gone, Toby keen to get an opinion on the documents that had come from Lizard, handed them to Arthur, who shared them with Charlie. Charlie studied them for a long time, then passed them back to him and tapping his finger on the solicitor's letter said, 'they're genuine alright. Looks like you have a bit of city real estate, young fella.'

Arthur slurped his tea and raised his eyebrow.

Charlie kept talking. 'You'll need to get probate granted before it's yours though. Outstanding land tax and rates might make it a white elephant too. What do you think Artie?'

'I don't know what to think, it's all a bit much.'

Sophia was bouncing the ring up and down in her palm.

'That's a problem though.' Arthur put his hand out and she gave it to him. 'If the story's true, then the further the ring is from here, the better.'

'Saul said he'd buy it anytime you wanted to sell,' Charlie said. 'Now I'd better make tracks. Just say if you want me to let Saul know you're interested, Tobe.'

'I'll think about it.' Toby said and turned Lizard's sketch book toward them. 'Here, look at this. He's drawn a dungeon and two skeletons. One is wearing the ring.'

'Let it rest until tomorrow, Tobe. We've had a big day and it's past my bedtime,' rising out of his chair Arthur said, 'C'mon Charlie, I'll walk you out.'

CHAPTER FIFTY-TWO

Toby stepped from the lift and seeing a throng of people, became curious. Someone was on the ground and security were moving in, pushing onlookers aside. Not far away Sophia was leaning with her back against the wall. Slasher, his hand flat palmed against it, trapped her there. The image triggered his rage. After the week he'd had and the conflict stirring inside him, his temper had reached bursting point. He smiled, now he could direct all that frustration at stinking Danny Sabo.

'Get away from her,' Toby was yelling, he felt eyes turning toward him and didn't care. 'Don't do it mate, because injured, or not, I'll drop you like a rock.'

'Toby, stop it, I'm okay,' scolding him, Sophia ducked out from under Slasher's arm and stood between them. 'Danny came to my rescue.'

Toby stared at them. 'So, it's *Danny* now?'

Danny Sabo held his hands up. 'I didn't do anything, Farrier. I only got here after Freckles gave her a slap.' He looked at Sophia and back to Toby, 'I held them back while she made him pay for it, that's all,' he said. Lifting his crutches, he pointed toward the cafeteria. 'Look, now that you've shot your big mouth off, there's people gawping at us everywhere, we'd better go into the café and find an empty corner,' he nudged Toby with his shoulder and smiling continued, 'and then I'll tell you how this little pocket rocket of yours turned Freckles inside out.'

'What happened out there?' Ben bounced up behind them, 'Freckle's not looking too good, is he?'

Toby heard the joy in his friend's voice. Ben saw Danny and his joy changed to a sneer. 'I thought you'd be out there with your mates, Creep?'

Danny shook his head. 'Not my gang... not anymore, anyway.' He nodded toward the throng and grinning said, 'Soph's one tough chick, spread Freckles like butter on hot toast.' and looking past Ben asked, 'Anyway, where's the rest of the posse, idiot?'

'Should be just behind me,' he answered. 'They couldn't wait to throw an insult or two at Freckles. He's been a proper pain in the butt ever since you made him boss.'

'He would,' he answered and reaching for his crutches said, 'come on Farrier, bring your mates and I'll tell you all about your little action woman here.' He used his sticks to hobble his way to the back of the room.

Listening to Danny describing how Sophia had subdued Freckles, filled Toby with pride and he remembered all the years Mrs Nguyen dragged her to karate lessons. The idiot should have known not to take her on. Sophia smiled and squeezed Toby's hand when Danny made the sucking sound of Freckle's shoulder dislocating. He left nothing out. Sophia had a fan.

Danny dropped his eyes and with his index finger started making invisible circles on the table, without looking he spoke to Toby. 'Mum says you came to see me a few times when I was out of it. Why?'

Toby, unable to look at him released Sophia's hand and made circles of his own, trying to find words that wouldn't sound trite. 'I don't know. Once I watched a movie called *Pay it Forward*. The message was strong. It might have been that. If I'm honest, I thought you could use a friend.' He nodded to where Freckles had lost his cred, 'I knew none of those idiots out there would visit and I had time.'

'Thanks, I'm sorry about the book too. This bloke said he was from ASIO and suckered me. Made me feel I was some kind of hero. You know, being a secret agent and all. All that James Bond stuff he talked about, got me in.'

Toby frowned. *ASIO?* Was this really an agent, someone other than the mad professor, or Phillip Ryan?

'More like Maxwell Smart,' Sophia said. She pushed at her hair on one side. 'You may call me... Ninety-Nine.'

Danny was staring at Toby's neck. 'Never saw you with jewellery before,' he said.

Rolling the ring between his fingers, Toby stretched out the cord enough for him to see it. 'Not usually my thing, I was given this by a bloke I met couple of days ago. Called himself Lizard.

'Nice, can I see?'

Toby knew if he really believed what he'd said about paying it forward, then this was his test. 'Yeah, why not...' lifting the cord over his head, he dropped the ring into Danny's palm.

Sophia reached for his hand and closing her fingers around it, kissed it.

Danny held the ring up to the light. 'Look Farrier, I have had a lot of time to think since I've been in here.' The light caught in the stone throwing a laser like spear of red light onto the wall. 'If I continue to buck the system and mix with the likes of Freckles and Parrot, I'm probably going to end up like my old man. I don't want that. I want to be more how Mum would like me to be,' he stared at Toby. 'It seems to me that I could do worse than ask you, your girlfriend here and your turnip mates, if you'd mind me kicking around with you?'

Toby stared at him.

'Why?' Ben, leaning over the table, stretched as close to Danny as he could and without standing asked, 'and why now Jerk? Only a week ago you couldn't wait to flush any one of us in the toilets. You were a proper arse, Sabo. And not just to those of us here, but plenty of other kids too.' Taking his time to sit back, Ben kept staring, holding his sneer.

'Yeah,' Jack jumped in, 'you couldn't wait to steal our lunch money, or pinch a magazine from any of us.' He mimicked Ben's pose; shoulders wide, arms spread and with his palms flat on the table, Jack looked bigger. 'And what? Now you want us to forget all of that, make out none of it happened.' Jack moved even closer and Danny backed away an inch, 'I don't think so, Sabo. You've got to do a whole lot more than just say you're sorry, before I'm ever likely to trust you.'

Nathan sat back watching and listening to what everyone was saying. At a break in the conversation, he pulled his chair in and leaned across the table. His hands were only millimetres from Slasher.

He locked onto Danny Sabo's eyes, 'something happened to land you in here, didn't it?' Nathan leant back in his chair clasping his hands behind his head. 'I heard you got belted, another rumour says a car hit you. Tell us what really happened, Danny. And then. Ask again.'

Danny started at the beginning. He told them about feeling Uncle Ralphie's fists as they pummelled him. How the disgust of his father still welled inside him, and how the man who was supposed to protect him, had kept his arms pinned to stop him getting away.

Sophia was rubbing Danny's arm, encouraging to go on.

Toby watched her. She smiled at him, he remembered her lips on his and smiled back.

Several times Danny looked away and bit his lip. No one interrupted and for minutes after he' finished telling his story, the table remained silent.

Toby watching his enemy's fingers wrapping and unwrapping, playing with the cord and feeling the ring, fought his desire to grab it. He knew if he were to make peace with Slasher it would be better to hold onto his emotions and turn his words into action, but it wasn't going to be easy.

Sophia kicked Toby's foot. She mouthed the words, *say something.*

Toby cleared his throat. 'Yeah, sorry... We didn't know it was like that. I don't know what to say,' he bit his tongue to stop him from adding, *and you can give my ring back now,* 'so what do we do now. We can't keep calling you Slash?'

'Call me what you like, Dan or Danny. Anything that marks a change'd be good'

Toby looked at each of his friends as he called their names, 'Sophia, Nathan, Ben, Jack?' pausing before asking, 'do we call him Dan?'

'God, I liked the way Slash just rolled off the tongue,' Ben said, and looking at his friends for confirmation, then turning to Slasher added, 'it's going to be damned hard, but okay, I guess I can try calling you Dan.'

'Jack?'

'Yeah, but one stuff up and he's out, Tobe.'

'Nathan, want to say something?'

'It's not going to be easy, but if Dan's willing to drop all the crap and make an effort to fit in, I'm okay with it. But we got together because he was a bully and I can't forget that either.' Nathan turned to Dan and waited a long few seconds before asking, 'can you maintain a truce... Dan?'

'Yeah, sure. I can,' he swallowed, 'I need to.'

Toby looked at Sophia, 'what about you Soph?'

'I reckon it's up to Danny, he has the most lose.'

'And the most to gain.' Danny replied.

As was their custom, everyone piled their hands one on top of each other's in the middle of the table. They waited for Dan to do the same. He hesitated, then putting his hand on the top of theirs said, 'Deal,'

'Done,' the friends said and waited a moment before pulling their hands away.

Toby put his hand out, 'my ring please.'

Dan looked at the cord around his fingers and unwrapped it. He raised his left hand high enough for the ring to swing above Toby's open palm. Toby fought the urge to snatch it as it made ever decreasing circles. Finally, Dan opened his fingers and Toby felt the ring drop into his hand.

'Bend forward,' Toby said.

'What?' Dan frowned.

'Bend forward you dipstick.' Toby smiled at him. 'It's fine, look just lean forward.'

Dan did as Toby asked.

'I want you to look after this until we get back from the city. Reckon you can do that?' Toby slipped the cord over Dan's head.

'Sure, what if Mum or someone asks where I got it?'

'Tell them, I got it from a dead man and you're holding it for me.' Toby was sure Dan would keep it safe for now. 'Tell them it's cursed.'

'Cool...' Danny looked at the ring one more time before tucking it under his shirt.

Sophia stood. 'We'd better go if we want to find this place of yours, Tobe.'

'Where?' Dan asked.

'The city, somewhere in Russell Street,' Ben said. 'A squat.'

'Can you hang onto this too?' Toby reached into his backpack and passed Dan the sketch book. 'Lizard gave it to me. I'll pick it up when we get back.'

CHAPTER FIFTY-THREE

Toby and his friends shouldered their backpacks and caught a tram into the city. They'd planned to start at Flinders Street and walk up to Russell Street, looking on both sides until they found it.

'That was a nice thing to do.' Sophia whispered as she squeezed Toby's hand.

'Probably pawned it by now, I'd reckon,' said Ben.

'I don't think so. Slash, I mean Dan'll keep it safe-and-sound,' she said in a sing-song way. 'You might need to take a leaf out of Toby's book from time to time, Benny.'

'Which book? Toby's got so many,' Jack skipped around and running backwards, said. 'Sheesh, I crack myself up at times.'

Nathan said he'd left his water bottle home and stopped at a cafe just past Collins Street. He came out with water and a chocolate bar. His friends milled around as he ripped open the bar's packet. Jack and Ben catching its scent decided they needed chocolate too and pushed through the shop door.

Toby's frustration boiled over, he followed them in and thrust a twenty dollar note in Jack's hand. 'Here, you might as well have a milkshake on me, I'm going ahead.' His friends thought they were on a picnic. He strode off down the road.

'What's all that about?' Sophia said as she caught up with him. 'They eat all the time, you know that.'

'I can't help it, sorry. I'm burnt up by Shamus, his desk and everything.' He pulled out the street map. It didn't make sense, there was nothing marked to indicate anything, anyone could use as a squat.

'Soph, the last few weeks have been full-on, up and down. I don't know what to think. At the hospital with Slasher, I mean Dan. Jeeze is that going to be hard to get used to—everything is upside down. I've had the family burst in on us, and carry on like they own the place. I get conned by a bloke to hold the hand of a dying man. Then he pops his clogs and leaves me a filthy squat I feel obliged to find. Who'd be in their right mind after all that's happened? Reckon we should pack this in and go home now. It's all bullshit anyway. Let's go as far as Victoria Street and then if we haven't found it, head home, okay?'

'Let's get to the top of Russell and we'll discuss it there,' she stepped ahead of him and skipped a couple of steps backward. 'Come on Toby, this is fun, we'll find it, you know we will.'

Jack, Nathan and Ben came pounding up behind them.

'Wow, Little Collins Street...Chinatown,' Jack said. 'Come on you two.' He skip-jumped into Melbourne's famous restaurant district and the others followed.

Toby stood on the corner and looked at Sophia. He opened his mouth to speak and she put her finger to his lips.

'Come on Tobe,' Ben called. 'We've always wanted to see Chinatown and we're here now, what have we got to lose?'

Sophia shrugged. 'We should never have had kids, they become uncontrollable as teenagers.'

She laughed and ran after them dragging Toby along with her.

'Just like you thought, Jack?' she asked, catching up to him.

'Better, and heaps better than a school trip too.'

CHAPTER FIFTY-FOUR

Toby looked at the solicitor's letter and back again to the street sign. 'Russell Place, no wonder we couldn't find it in Russell Street Soph, It's the old electric substation down here, come on.'

'We should wait for the others, yeah?' she said.

'I reckon I can see it.' He ran off and called to her. 'You find them and I'll open the place up.' He waved the key at her and winked. 'Probably needs a bit of an airing.'

The key slid into the well-worn padlock and with an easy twist opened. Toby, pulled the door open and not wanting to be locked in by accident, clicked the lock closed again. The others caught up with him and they stood at the entrance.

'Phew,' Sophia pinched her nose, 'it stinks like someone's been using it for toilet.

Toby stepped inside, it was dark and seeing a row of steps leading skyward, turned his backpack toward Sophia, 'Can you find my torch for me please?'

'Better than that,' she said, 'I'll try this switch, shall I?'

Above them light flowed down from a sculpture high in the atrium. Small discs of amber light lit each tread of the stairs.

'Smarty,' he said.

On the floor, a mural of an emerald green gecko with glowing red eyes caused him to look down. Satanic red on black images directed his eyes to a staircase winding its way down to another level. Someone had painted the hand rail to resemble lava.

'You okay?' he asked her.

'Come on let's do this and get out of here.'

'I can hear the others, come on,' and reaching for her hand thought he felt the hair on his neck stand up. If it wasn't for the others with him, he'd have turned around and run out of this place.

'Wow how cool is this?' Nathan was egging the gang on, but as they got lower down, the talking stopped.

A line of painted red coals guided them deeper and they changed shape the further they went. Stars started to appear around them, as they crept lower.

Ben, his voice shaking asked, 'How much further Toby, I reckon we ought to think about turning back soon.'

Toby studied the painted coals on the wall. Soon they became rubies and the stars took the shape of cut diamonds and the stairwell became darker. Feeling his way along the hand rail, he saw its colour change to gold. His head and heart raced. What was this place?

Hearing a door slam above them, Toby held his hand up to stop the group moving. He felt his heart thumping so hard that he thought the others would hear it. Again, a voice, or something other than human echoed down the stairs.

'Shush,'

'You guys hear that, too?' Ben's question was barely a whisper.

Sophia grabbed Toby's hand, her nails digging into his palm.

'It's nothing,' Toby said, hoping they couldn't hear the shake in his voice. 'Anyway, we're here now.'

The room was black and only the faint light coming from the stairs gave them any sense to their location.

Turning his torch on he saw that they were now inside a tall, cylindrical room and standing on a chequer plate steel floor. Finding a hatch, Toby opened it. Dropping onto his tummy and sticking his head into the abys his eyes searched the torchlight. Finding a light brass chain, he tugged on it. A light under the floor sent hundreds of tiny beams skyward. All different colours the lights danced like flames licking at anything in their path.

'Wow that's really cool,' he said and looked at the beams casting light and shadow to the top of the chamber. 'We can party down here and no one'll hear us.'

'Yeah, Nathan added, 'and we could write on the invites *To Hell with the Party.*'

'It's giving me the creeps,' Sophia said tugging on Toby's sleeve, 'I'm scared and I reckon we should get out of here.'

Toby thought he'd seen something further below the hatch, 'You lot stay here, I'll go down the ladder for a bit to see what's there. If I find something, I'll give you a shout, but you better come down one at a time, can't be too sure of this ladder.' Toby shed his backpack and prepared to descend.

Jack dropped onto his stomach and peered down the hole, then moved aside. Toby climbed in and felt his way down. The ladder was steel and the rungs were about thirty centimetres apart. At five metres a platform with handrails jutted across to the wall. Toby found the ladder continued through a hole in the platform, wriggled through and followed it deeper. He could hear water. It was a well. Staring down and unable to see anything else, he decided to climb up again.

Twisting his way back through the hole of the platform, his torchlight revealed another hatch made from a metal plate. It had a hinge and was folded back on itself. It was made to cover the ladder opening. He stepped onto the platform, lifted the hatch over centre and let it drop. The sound ringing in his ears as it echoed against the water.

'Toby, are you alright?' Sophia yelled down.

He shouted back that he was okay.

'I'm getting out of here, 'She said, 'and you should come too,' Toby could hear the tremble in her voice.

'Two minutes, and then I'm coming up, okay?' he called back.

'I'm counting you down,' she said.

Toby crawled across the platform, testing every step. His fingers scoured the bricks. Why would anyone put a landing across here? Bridges like this had to go somewhere. He stretched on tip toes and couldn't find a crack to define an opening. He felt his torch slipping, and tried to secure it, it was all that was between him feeling okay, or feeling like he was stuck in a very dark place. The strap clicked open, it fell forward and rattled on the steel floor. The beam showed a scrape mark meaning there was a door and it had to swing out. He traced the dragline and found an edge. The door was steel and textured to merge with the bricks making it disappear into the wall. Without a handle, he knew there had to be a trigger and exploring the hand rail with his fingers found a tubular slip sleeve.

Dragging the sleeve toward the ladder exposed a split tube that formed half of the rail. Toby lifted and the door sprung toward him about a centimetre. He pulled on its edge. The door was heavy and as thick as the wall. His light searched the opening and sought out the round brass of an ancient switch. He flicked it.

'Hey,' he shouted up to his friends, 'You guys should come down here and see this, there's a whole other room in here.'

Once he heard them coming down the ladder, he made his way further into a chamber that opened into a brick lined room. In the gloom, he felt for another switch.

'Wow, this is different,' Ben said, cupped his hands to his mouth and yelled up to the others. 'You guys should see this,'

Jack came through next, then Nathan.

'Soph's not coming down,' Nathan told him, 'she's frightened Tobe. And you did say two minutes.'

'Yeah, I know, just a quick look and then we are out of here, yeah?'

He found a row of switches. The room yellowed with incandescent light.

Ben screamed.

'What is it?' Sophia yelled.

'There's a dead guy in here,' Ben yelled back.

'One dead guy? There are two dead guys in here.' Jack's voice was hysterical, 'come on, we should get outta here.'

'We're coming out now,' Toby called up to her, 'just hang in there a little longer, okay? He took a couple of photos with his phone, the blast of the flash blinded him for a minute.

He heard Sophia squealing, and then she was quiet.

'Soph, Soph?' Toby held his hand out, indicating for the others to be quiet. 'Sophia? Are you all right?' All he could hear was the sound of his heart pounding. 'Answer me, Soph, please?'

The ladder started ringing with the footfall of hard soled shoes. Toby felt sick. Why wasn't she replying? Something was wrong. She would reply if it was her coming down the ladder. What if it was someone else? What if it was the creepy professor? He pointed to the outer room and all four of them crept into it. The footsteps were on the landing now and moving toward them. Toby killed the lights where they were hiding, but kept the skeletons illuminated. Light caught the ruby in the gunman's ring and it sent spears of red across the floor. Sensing the owner of the footsteps was close enough to touch them they flattened themselves against the wall.

Toby held a finger to his lips and the shadow brushed past them it was the professor and he looked to be mesmerised, his eyes focussed on the skeleton with the ruby ring. Toby motioned for the others to leave and when they were clear, cut the lights and ran out of the room slamming the door behind him. Toby could hear the professor screaming behind the door. making sure it was locked he followed the others up the ladder.

At the top of the ladder flashlights were flicking around. The staircase was full of people.

'Over here.'

Toby recognised that voice. Mr Wyatt.

Sophia's scarf had been tied around her mouth. Their teacher's fingers were pinching and pulling at the twine wrapped around her hands and ankles, trying to free her. The others were milling around, everyone talking at once. The two police officers stepped into the light.

Toby rushed over and pulled the scarf away. 'I'm sorry, Soph, so sorry,' He dropped to his knees and hugged her.

Pushing him away she searched his eyes for answers. 'Where is he?' 'He attacked me again. I know it was him. It's the same bloke who attacked me before.' She saw the policeman and turning to John pleaded. 'Get him please, I just want you to get him...'

Jenny held her hand out and helped Sophia up. 'Let's get you out of here.' She led Sophia to the stairs encouraging her to climb out.

Looking at Toby and pointing at the hatch, John said, 'where is he, down there?'

Toby nodded.

'And William? What are you doing here?' John's voice was stern. 'Looking for your brother?'

Mr Wyatt nodded.

'Brother?' Toby said.

'Yes Toby, he's my brother. Sorry, when I saw some of the sketches and the ring you left with Danny today,' the teacher looked from Toby to John, 'I put two and two together and thought I'd better start looking for the kids. Phillip's become unhinged.' He looked back to where Toby and the others were standing. 'Are you all here? Roll call.'

'Nathan, Sir.'

'Toby.'

'Ben.'

'Jack'.

John turned to Toby. 'Is it Professor Phillip Ryan down there?'

'I don't know,' Toby said, 'but what I do know, is that the creep down there is the same bloke who slapped me in the street. The same guy who belted me back at Pop's and the same guy who attacked Sophia on her way home. I'm damned sure he's the turd who broke into Pop's house too. And if he dies down there, then he'll only be one more corpse in a very dark room. After what he's put everyone through, I can live with that.'

John held his shoulders and looked in his eyes. 'We have to get him out of there.'

Toby turned to his teacher. 'I'm sorry Sir. I don't care if he is your brother, but he's one evil bastard.' He turned back to John. 'The police couldn't hold him, but I can.' He kicked the trapdoor shut. 'If he rots down there, too bad, and I think Larry the Lizard would even approve.' He stood on the cover plate. 'If things get too tough for him, he can always take the gun from the skeleton, and put himself out of his misery.'

John dragged him away from the trapdoor. 'Toby if you mean that, then you're no better than he is. Think of all the stuff you'll do in the next few years. Think of Sophia, would she be happy if he dies down there? It'll kill your Pop, Tracy, Darren, the girls and these blokes, what about them?' John hugged him. 'Jeez, Tobe, you've come too far to let a creep like him ruin you. Tell me how it works down there, and I'll take care of it.'

Toby nodded and looked at his mates. 'But you blokes have to go.'

'Right you lot, upstairs.' John said. 'Will, you see how Soph's doing, and get Jenny to call for armed response.' No one moved. 'Out of here now. Go'

Toby was down the ladder first. The flap was still over the bridge. John crept past him on the landing and moved behind the door. Toby sprung the lock. As the door opened, Toby heard a man sobbing.

Professor Phillip Ryan sat alongside the gunman's skeleton, tears streaked his cheeks and his mumbling was incomprehensible. Once in a while Toby thought he heard him say something like, *I found you, Great Granddad I found you.*

John moved to the other side of the skeleton and took the gun from its hand and the knife from its chest. He pulled Ryan to his feet and turned him against the wall. In one practiced movement, he snapped Ryan's wrists into the hand cuffs.

'Toby, I have things under control here.' He was breathing deeply. 'Well done mate, you've found evidence of two very old murders. Now go upstairs and wait, okay?'

'Yeah, are you going to be okay down here?' Toby flicked the other lights on.

'Sure, you get up there and take care of your girlfriend.'

Toby turned to leave and stopped. 'The latch to open the door from this side is here. I guess Ryan didn't find it. Lucky, that?' Toby sprinted to the ladder.

John shouted out, 'Send Mr Wyatt down as soon he can make it.'

'Will do.'

Police streamed into the building as Toby reached the top of the stairs.

'Constable Evans has it all under control. Take care on the ladder it's old.'

'Sure, kid, thanks.' Jenny high-fived him.

CHAPTER FIFTY-FIVE

John explained to Toby and his family that the police were preparing a case to declare Phillip Ryan criminally insane. Psychiatrists had concluded he was too mentally unwell to face trial and believed the court would accept their recommendation to place him into a secure facility for the rest of his life.

'You say, rest of his life,' Sophia said, 'but we all know that judges set a minimum time for parole and then murderers get out early. I don't want him ever coming after me again.'

'This is quite different; a panel of doctors will review his mental state at regular intervals,' John said. 'But it might be better if Will tells you a bit more about him.

Will sighed before he started talking. 'My brother will be no trouble to you, Sophia. It seems the Gypsies' Curse has found us again. Phillip has an aggressive brain tumour. He'll be lucky to live more than twelve months. The doctors say that it probably explains some of his behaviour. He received the results of an MRI confirming the disease three months ago, but kept it to himself.'

'A tumour?' Sophia said. 'Are you sure?'

Mr Wyatt nodded. 'I think he was convinced if he found Great Grandfather's ring and returned it to the gypsies' family it would cure him. I went through his notes and found the family. They've no record of ever owning such a ring. So, I've got no idea where this story of a curse came from. I wish he'd never heard of it.'

When Will paused John said, 'We're still doing tests, but the DNA results of the skeleton we think is Bill Ryan, doesn't match either Phillip or Will. The other skeleton is a small-time crook who ran errands for John "Snowy" Cutmore. The deposit boxes are full of gold, cash and precious stones. We found a couple of interesting weapons and one box had a skull in it.'

'What happens to that?' Ben said.

'The skull?' John asked.

'No, all of it?'

'We'll work that out when it's identified. For now, you should consider everything as *ill gotten gains*, and surrendered to the State. That's about all I can tell you now.'

'I know I've had enough excitement for one week,' Arthur said. 'And I think the same goes for everyone. John, Jenny, I'd like to thank you for sticking with us through this. Will, I'm sorry your brother is ill, but I'll sleep better tonight, knowing that he's under lock and key.' He put an arm around Toby. 'If I have forgotten anybody, please don't take offence. I appreciate all of you.' He looked at Toby. 'You might put all of this in a book one day and make us famous.'

'Who knows?' Toby said and broke away.

Arthur winked and pointed at Charlie. 'Charlie Rankin, I blame you. If you had kept Shamus O'Toole and his damn desk hidden, none of us would have gone through this.' He laughed at the sad face Charlie pulled. 'Thanks mate, where would we be without you.'

The group began to laugh, Arthur called above the crowd. 'Family, to your rooms, the rest of you are dismissed. For now, I need to focus my efforts on Darren. Thank you and good night.'

Toby lay on his bed rubbing the pages Jazz had screwed up. Sophia moved to his side and wriggled alongside him.

'Tracy gave me some Clearasil,' he said.

'She told me. What are you doing?'

'I'm trying to work out what's on this page, but it's crumpled and I can't tell.'

'I can fix that.' She stood up and pulled his hand. 'Come to the laundry.'

'What?'

'Remember what Tracy told us she did with her homework.' She took the paper, turned the iron on and set it to dry. 'I'm going to iron it.'

'Test a corner to make sure we don't damage it.' The page started to smooth, and brown words began to appear. It was a letter. The hand writing was exquisite.

'A woman wrote this, Toby. No man could be that neat. It is part of a love letter.'

'Smell that? Lemon.' Toby sniffed. 'They used lemon juice as invisible ink. That is why the pen was sticky and smelled of lemon when Tracy threw it at me.' He kissed her. 'You are a genius girlfriend, a genius.

It took the best part of two hours to iron the letters. He thought about the method Shamus had used to hide the words. Arthur still used a spray bottle of water instead of steam when he ironed his shirts. Toby had taken it from the window sill and sprayed the corner of one page. The paper wrinkled and in seconds the words had vanished. They could now read the letters and moved to his bedroom to sort them.

In his room and trying to sort the letters they heard Tracy come home and drop her handbag and keys on the bench.

She crept into Toby's room, 'what are you two up to?' she said shutting the door

'How's Dad?'

'Most of the tubes are out, but he still can't talk. All his limbs are moving and he has feeling in every finger and toe. He's back.' Tracy glowed and looked more beautiful than she ever had.

She held Sophia's hands and looked into her eyes. 'Another bit of good news for us girls, I had a call from a modelling friend and she has tickets for me and you to go to Fashion Week. I asked her to get one for your mum too, think she'd like to come.' She wiggled and squealed. 'Fashion Week.'

She took the letter Toby held out. 'These are from...Zeta to Shamus. Whoever Zeta is. Love letters?'

'We were trying to sort them into some order, but we started reading them instead.' Sophia passed Tracy a pile. 'Want to help?'

'Are they gossipy?'

'She's married, and having an affair,' Soph said.

'Let me at them then.' Squash up, she tried to squeeze down beside them. It was too narrow. 'C'mon, bring this lot into my room.'

For nearly an hour they ploughed through the pages. Tracy and Sophia were giggling.

Tracy pointed to a sentence on a page and nudged Sophia with her elbow. 'Mrs Zeta Ryan, wife of William Ryan, the banker. Willy's Great Grand Mama was pregnant by Toby's private eye.'

Sophia sifted through the papers. 'Got it.' She held the page aloft and waved it in front of Toby's nose. 'Twice, she says here that William is a brute, and she would love to be rid of him.' Soph shuffled the pages for a moment then pulled one out. 'Here. Listen to this: *Shamus, your son is a magnificent young fellow, he will be heir to all of this one day, and even so, I'm doomed to live a life of deceit.*'

'Hey, I have more,' Toby said, 'she says here that William saw the ring she bought for Shamus. He quizzed her on it and she said it was a Father's Day present. Zeta snatched it before William could get a good look at it. She'll give it to Shamus the next time they meet.

'You reckon you have something, listen to this.' Tracy said. 'She was devious, old Zeta. She writes: *Since my husband has disappeared, his cronies are lining up for a piece of me every day. I have had the lawyers chase them off and I may need your help.*

'*In the meantime, I have told anyone who will listen that a gypsy put a hex on him for foreclosing on her, and that as long as he has the ring, the family is cursed. Within a week, the story had rumbled around the household staff and I'm sure half of Melbourne will know the story now.*' Tracy put the page on her lap. 'The old witch, I do like her style.'

'Wait, there's more,' Sophia said. 'Here she goes again: *Shamus, I blame William for the death of our daughter. I know he was nowhere near the house when she drowned, but in my mind, it was him. He built the fountain too deep.*'

Toby thought for a minute. 'If they only had three children and the girls died, then the next William Ryan is not a Ryan, but an O'Toole. Shamus O'Toole dies and his ring ends up with Larry the Lizard O'Toole, who has a squat with the dead William Ryan in it.' Toby wriggled to put his back against the headboard. 'That's why the DNA doesn't match Chalkie's. He's descended from Shamus. Brilliant, that is bloody brilliant.'

'And since Dan proved he could be trusted, you still have Lizard O'Toole's ring on a dirty cord around your neck, Toby.' Tracy leant up on one elbow and tickled him. 'And it's got Lizard's DNA all over it. What do you think of the chances?'

'Stop it.' Toby squirmed.

'I think we should ask John to test it.' He giggled when she tickled him again. 'I think both Larry and Shamus would like that. It seems both were forgotten until now.'

'Right you two, it's after midnight, and tomorrow I've got to get my fitness regime back on track.' She slid off the bed and sashayed around the room. 'Three months and then...*I'm going to take my little turn on the catwalk, on the catwalk. I'm too sexy...*' She sang and danced, then turned to them. 'Now you two out. Toby, you better walk Sophia straight home,' she pretended to look coy, 'and don't do anything that people may allege, I have done.'

As Toby left the house, he heard the shower running and Tracy singing the, *I'm Too Sexy,* song.

He held Sophia's hand until they reached her front door. 'Can you believe it, Soph, we solved it. The letters we found, why the pen was full of lemon juice, evidence to prove Larry and Shamus were related and, we helped catch a demented professor. We did all that. You and me,' Toby leant in to her. 'God, it feels so good, I could kiss you.'

'I'm not stopping you,' she whispered.

About the Author

Born in Orroroo, South Australia, Terry L Probert ran a successful motor business until joining AGCO Massey Ferguson in1996 and working in sales and marketing roles within the tractor and machinery industry for the next decade. Diagnosed with muscular dystrophy in 2012 he decided to change focus and put those skills into fiction writing.

Today he and his wife Ruth call Bendigo home and when adventure calls, they travel across Australia seeking locations and different characters for new novels.

Writing Achievements:

- 2013 Banib the Bunyip - Second City of Melton Short Story Competition

- 2015 Teenage Summer – Short Story published in Australian Writer

BOOKS

- 2013 KUNDELA – "Commended" Christina Stead Awards

- 2017 Voss: The Price of Innocence

- 2019 Gillespie's Gold

- 2022 Ian O'Rourke, Memories of a Tractor Man

- 2022 Noel - An Authorised Memoir